T0102882

Heart Mountain

"Home on the Ranch"

Radine Banks

A special thanks to Duane Schoffer who so appropriately blended 2 photos to create the beautiful cover for my book. Many heartfelt thanks to you, Duane.

Order this book online at www.trafford.com
or email orders@trafford.com

Most Trafford titles are also available at major online book retailers.

Note for Librarians: A cataloguing record for this book is available from Library
and Archives Canada at www.collectionscanada.ca/amicus/index-e.html

Printed in Victoria, BC, Canada.

ISBN: 978-1-4269-0192-8 (soft)
ISBN: 978-1-4269-0194-2 (ebook)

*We at Trafford believe that it is the responsibility of us all, as both individuals
and corporations, to make choices that are environmentally and socially sound.
You, in turn, are supporting this responsible conduct each time you purchase a
Trafford book, or make use of our publishing services. To find out how you are
helping, please visit www.trafford.com/responsiblepublishing.html*

*Our mission is to efficiently provide the world's finest, most comprehensive
book publishing service, enabling every author to experience success.
To find out how to publish your book, your way, and have it available
worldwide, visit us online at www.trafford.com*

Trafford rev. 7/16/2009

 www.trafford.com

North America & international
toll-free: 1 888 232 4444 (USA & Canada)
phone: 250 383 6864 ♦ fax: 250 383 6804 ♦ email: info@trafford.com

The United Kingdom & Europe
phone: +44 (0)1865 487 395 ♦ local rate: 0845 230 9601
facsimile: +44 (0)1865 481 507 ♦ email: info.uk@trafford.com

To my Readers:

Memory is a way of holding on to the things you love, the things you are, and the things you never want to lose.

I am pleased to say that a large part of what you will read in these pages is from memories that come flooding through my mind. Memories of the many happy times I spent during the years I lived on the ranch; includng the hardships of homesteading, giving birth to five wonderful children, and developing life-long friendships. As you turn the pages my hope is that you will find yourself walking beside me as we travel down my road of memories.

This book was written for my children:

Bill the rancher

Bob, the preacher

Gary, aeronautical consultant

Roger , electrician: and my crutch , always by my side

Last but certainly not least, my daughter, and editor whose unwavering confidence and encouragement brought me to the end of my story.

Thanks you so very much Patti.

I would like to thank Don Silvius and Benny De La Cruz for their unwavering confidence in my writing ability to continue writing; therefore turning my first novel, "Nochi" into a trilogy. Also thanks to Alicia DeLaurie for her sincerity and helpfulness during the writing of the "Heart Mountain."

Chapter 1
CARLA

I HAD CRIED until tears no longer came. Nochi was dead. My beautiful Nochi was dead. I am still in shock, even though I knew he was very sick, I never let myself believe that he would actually be gone. We buried him beneath the large Oak tree near the back pasture where we spent so many wonderful times together. Nochi grazing on the fresh green grass, and me lying in the shade, of the big oak tree, daydreaming. Nochi had been a big part of my life since I was about four years old. Of course I had ridden since I could remember, but my father was always there with me. He saddled Nochi, then helped me into the saddle. He would take the reins and lead me around the coral. This time I was told to do everything myself. I threw the blanket over his back, then with a great deal of effort, I finally placed the saddle on his back.

I remember how excited I was to ride down the lane that led to the old oak tree Nochi grazed on the fresh green grass and I dreamed as boys do; about races we would enter, about school and maybe even a girlfriend.

That is all ended now, and I realized I must tell Carla about Nochi's death. Carla and I had been friends about two years. Carla was sixteen and I was seventeen. Many things had happened in the past two years. My fingers shook while I was trying to call Carla. She answered on the second ring. I was relieved, as I probably would have hung up, because I hated the thought of bringing the bad news of Nochi's death to someone as close as Carla and I had become during these past few months. When she answered; hearing her voice seemed to calm me down a bit and I was able to speak without my voice sounding squeaky or shaky. Carla had her own horse, Sapphire, but I knew how much she loved Nochi. I remember how bad she felt when Nochi was injured in the barn fire. I could always depend her to calm me down when I was upset. I remember the time my math teacher accused me of using a calculator on a test. I was very upset that the teacher did not trust me. When I told Carla about it, she said, "Mark you and I both know you did not use a calculator. Tell Mr. Jenkins the truth tomorrow after class and then forget it." I ended up making a B+ in the class. I could hear her quiet sobbing on the phone. I knew she was crying, because she had become very attached to Nochi the past two years. When she was able to speak again she said, "I loved Nochi as if he was my own. All I can say is you will have to get another horse. In the meantime you can ride Sapphire. We will be partners raising our colt.

You are actually part owner. It is only fair that you have half interest in Harmony since Nochi was the sire."

Many things had happened in the past two years. Most important was the birth of Nochi and Sapphire's colt, Harmony. Carla and I both loved Harmony very much. She was a beautiful colt, and would be a beautiful mare. "Remember when we decided on Harmony as a name for Nochi and Sapphire's colt?" "I sure do," I said "I thought your idea for Harmony was perfect, since Harmony in music means a combination of two notes, and Sapphire's colt is sired by Nochi. Sapphire and Nochi mean Harmony. Very good thinking Carla." I knew exactly when I hung the receiver up, why I needed to hear Carla's voice. Carla and I were both seniors. I was one year older than Carla, because my birthday was in December and her birthday was in April. Consequently, she started to school a year before I did. She will graduate at sixteen, but I will be seventeen. Our senior year had been fun. We attended the Prom, went on field trips, and chalked up lots of good memories. Now it was time for College. Because of her excellent grades, Carla received a scholarship to attend Montana State University, and I decided to attend a College near home. This meant that Carla and I would only see each other two, maybe three times each year. I was dreading this separation, as our friendship was built on mutual interests, coupled with admiration and actually a sort of dependence. We both realized that we could no longer pick up the phone on a whim and talk about problems that we had experienced during the day, nor could we share small pleasures. We would be very busy with studies, new friendships, or just plain everyday happenings as we were in the habit of doing. I planned on helping Carla's parents care for Sapphire and Harmony. Since I continued living at home, I was also responsible for many chores on the ranch.

We wished each other good luck and promised to write or call as often as time permitted. Saying good-bye to a special friend like Carla was saddening and I was in a down mood for days afterward. I tried to concentrate on getting enrolled in my chosen classes in college, visiting Sapphire and Harmony as often as possible, and helping my father bring in the fall crops. I was planning on a career in agriculture as that was the only life I knew. I loved my parents and the life they had given me. I felt a great deal of admiration for my parents. Especially the tough road they had traveled to see their dreams fulfilled. A lovely home, with hundreds of acres of farmland on which to produce a comfortable living. If I followed the example they laid for me, I could have a successful life both financially and enjoyable. By taking agriculture in college, I would learn many new scientific advances which I could apply to my own ranch business of cattle and crops.

The story of my parent's experiences from the start to where they were now was so interesting and inspirational that I often suggested they write a book or at least keep an accurate log, so that someday their experiences could be shared with many other people. I knew without a doubt that family and friends everywhere would find the experiences of my parents homesteading days as interesting as I did. Without my knowledge, mother, and I am sure with help from my father, had actually kept an account of those days and had written a book, which I had suggested several years back. Now, that I was on my way to college, Mom decided the proper time had come to surprise my sister, Kati and I by sharing her long kept secret with us. I was thrilled beyond words to know that she had made the decision to write. It was not a large book and I was eager to read it. I started reading and in spite of my sleepy eyes, I read to the end. She began the book like this: I am dedicating this story of our Homesteading days to my precious children, Mark and Kati. To my husband who helped me remember important events, and last but not least to my loving father for suggesting the idea. Without his constant urging, we would never have entered the drawing for the land that the Government was giving away. We took the necessary steps, filed the papers to enter the drawing, then went on with our daily routine; never dreaming that we might win. We had satisfied my fathers wishes; made him happy and considered that to be the end of an outrageous idea.

Chapter 2
HOMESTEADING

IT WAS the year 1950; We had been living in Denver, Colorado, and were getting ready to buy a home, when one day to my surprise, my husband came home from his job as a car mechanic and announced that we would be moving to Boise, Idaho. My husband was one of those people who thought "the grass was greener on the other side." I loved my husband very much and was willing to move to Boise or anywhere just to be with him. We made the move to Boise, settled in a less than desirable apartment, and started life all over again until another surprise came, which really did turn our lives around. We received a message informing us that we had actually won a large piece of land in Wyoming through the government lottery we had filed paper to enter while we were in living in Denver,Colorado. We were shocked out of our minds to say the least! Neither of us had been to Wyoming, and had no idea what to expect. We were to choose the piece of land we wanted .After inquiring further, we learned that we could turn our land down and it would go to the next person in line, or we could accept the land, live on it for a period of two years, then sell it, which would bring us more money than we had ever dreamed of saving up. We accepted our lucky winnings, and began the process of signing the necessary papers to close the deal. We were required to have two thousand dollars cash in the bank. Where in the world would we get that much cash. Your father had about one thousand in a retirement fund, but where would the remaining one-thousand come from. My father, of course. We asked him for the thousand we needed, and after talking to his banker, he handed us the extra thousand we needed to close the deal. Dear ole Dad was always there when we needed him. We promised to pay him back when the first crop was sold. never knowing just when that might be . It might be never!

Mark our 1st born child was now about three years old We left our precious little boy with his grandmother in Vernal, Utah and headed for the wide open spaces of Wyoming.

We reached Cody, WY late in the afternoon, and marveled at the georgous sunset and the magnificent mountains in the horizon. One mountain especially caught our eye. When we ask locals about it, they said it was called, "Heart Mountain" I think we fell in love with our new home before sunset the following day. We drove out to the area which appeared to be nothing but wide open spaces, with the blowing tumble weeds in front of our car, and roads that were narrow; just barely wide enough for two cars to pass. We choose a place we felt was the best farmland.

Feeling adventurous and happy with our newly acquired land, we decided to drive further down the valley for a little more sightseeing. I mentioned to your father that the weather was getting cloudy and looked like a storm brewing. He didn't think it looked bad enough to turn and go back, so being the greenhorns we were, we kept driving. Soon after our conversation about the weather, the wind picked up and snow began to fall. We did not realize that we were driving in a blizzard. Natives of Wyoming would never let themselves get caught in such a storm. We drove on thinking we would soon be on a more traveled road, but instead we ran into a place where snow had drifted across the road and we were stalled. We were certainly not dressed for walking, but decided we should leave the car and walk. We walked in one direction, but the wind was blowing much too hard to continue in that direction, so we turned and walked with our backs to the wind. We could see no buildings in the distance and we were freezing cold. The temperature must have been ten degrees below zero, and the wind blowing at least fifteen miles per hour At last we spotted a shack about one half mile away. Your father suggested that I take refuge, out of the storm while he went ahead hoping to find help.   I refused to stay alone; thinking if I was going to freeze to death I did not want to do it alone, so on we went. It was almost dark and my feet had no feeling left in them. I had worn sandals with no socks, a light jacket, with nothing on my head to protect me from the blowing snow and wind. When we left our motel that morning, I never dreamed I would be walking in a storm. Finally we saw a light in the distance,which was a total surprise, because we had actually given up; thinking we might freeze to death in this terrible weather. We arrived at the house and were welcomed with open arms. The people living there had come about two months earlier, chosen their place and had a comfortable cabin. They were very hospitable. They served us dinner, a nice warm bed, and breakfast. After spending the night there, our host took his tractor and pulled us out of the snow drift.

During our stay with these lovely people, we found that they were natives of Wyoming and told us of numerous times when locals had actually frozen to death in storms such as we were in. Now we knew what a wild, but beautiful country we had chosen to be our home!

The government had given each homesteader a barracks that had been used to house Japanese in an internment camp during WW11. When the Japanese bombed the U.S. and we were at War with Japan, the government placed all Japanese living in this country in camps. The camps were located all over the United States, and one was built in Wyoming, about five miles from our homestead. Of course, by the 1950's no prisoners were living in the camp, and the buildings were not in use, so the government gave them to homsteaders. These buildings were very old, but they served as homes for the homesteaders until enough money could be saved to build houses. We were very thankful to the government for furnishing us a home. Some people who homesteaded had enough money to build a house, but most of us used the barracks, as they were called.

When we were ready to move into our barracks, I had to sweep snow out of what was to be our bedroom before we could set the bed up. Snow had drifted in through the loose windows. The next job was to tighten those windows up! Of course, eating out was out of the question, because of money and cafes were too far away. We were furnished a large coal stove, called a "warm morning heater", which served for heat and cooking. I was too far away from a store to buy a loaf of bread so I actually baked biscuits on the top of the old "warm morning heater." I certainly had to use my ingenuity during those very tough times. We had no electricity or water available, so we used kerosene lanterns for light and hauled water from the nearby Japanese internment camp. We used an old fashioned toilet or outhouse for a bathroom, and took all our baths in a large washtub.

My husband, along with all the other homesteaders, attended a government school three times each week. When he went to school to learn about farming, I was left alone in this strange place. When I turned my lantern out to go to bed I had no light until your father returned from his class.We had no newspaper, television, or radio. The evenings were long and lonely. I was very thankful for my young son to keep me company.

After a few weeks, I became acquainted with some neighbor ladies and we enjoyed getting together for cards on school nights. We enjoyed playing cards and getting to know one another. We eventually became close friends and neighbors.

Neighbors were very important and we became very close in a short time. Most people did not have family living near, so we helped each other. We listened to problems a neighbor might have and tried to comfort them in any way we could. One of the most tragic things that happened was the drowning of a child. A young son of one of the neighbors wandered away from his house to one of the many canals that ran alongside a main road. These canals were often very close to yards where children played. The water ran swift . So much so that children were warned not to go near a canal. The child that drowned was only four years old, and as children often do, he left his front yard, went to the canal, got too close to the swift water, fell into the swift water and drowned. Of course the parents were devastated to the point that they simply could not carry on with the field work and chores they needed to do. Neighbors pitched in with field work and chores. We women brought food to their home, comforted the family and did many things to show our concern and sympathy.

Another time, a child ran out into the road and was hit by a car and was killed. As was the custom, everyone showed the family much kindness. Children in those days had more space to run in and often met with trouble.

We were young and played as well as worked together. We organized a community club for recreational things. We held pot-lucks, dances and anything that required a get-together. We upgraded an old barracks like the ones we used for homes, and the men put a new roof on, repaired the windows, while we ladies hung curtains, equipped the kitchen, and covered the floors with linoleum . When we were finished we celebrated with a special pot-luck dinner and dance.

As I have said, we had very little money, but we thought if we were going to be farmers we would need some animals around, so we took part of our meager savings and bought a cow, a couple of pigs and a few chickens. Now we were actually real farmers. I remember the day our "John Deere Tractor" was delivered. Your father had never been on a tractor. He climbed up into the seat and started the motor. He stepped on the gas pedal and took off. I was terrified he would run into the shack we called our barn. I even imagined he might hit our cow and pigs, but he managed to turn that strange machine around and finally stopped a few feet from where he started. After the tractor, we bought a few more pieces of machinery and began planting our very first crop. Peas was our first crop. After they were harvested they were sold as seed peas. The one job I refused to do on the farm was milk that nasty cow. The years passed and I stayed with my conviction, not to mess with that cow. Luckily, my husband had learned to milk a cow, as his family had a cow when he was a boy. I was more than willing to help with other outdoor jobs as the years passed.

One time that stands out in my memory was a time when I was called on to hold some baby lambs while my husband put a rubber band around their tails. Eventually they would lose their tails. Before we ever left the city for this wild country, I had sworn to keep my skin in nice shape, which meant putting cream on my face before going to the corral to perform whatever job I was asked to do. The wind was blowing, as it does in Wyoming. This day was no different. I held the lambs, we finished the job and I went to the house. When I looked in the mirror, I saw my face and started screaming. My face was covered with cow dung. The wind had blown the stuff onto my lovely skin and it stuck there. Needless to I say, I washed my face many times before I felt that my skin was clean again. That incident proved to be one of the many times I would have sold the farm in a minute for one dollar or even given it away. These and many other memories will be in my mind if I live to be ninety years old.

We were very blessed that none of the disasters that many people experienced happened to us. Many homesteaders were hit by hail storms. Often the wind blew so fiercely, that it blew silos and even barns away. We continued our success and bought more and more land to go along with the homestead.

After two years of living without modern conveniences, the federal government furnished us with electricity and we were able to live a normal life. We had a water well dug, and no longer had to use the outhouse. We actually had a nice bathroom.

After all my prayers I had a baby girl. We called her Kati. Kati was a beautifu child. She was blessed with deep blue eyes, and gorgeous red hair.

This is only a tiny bit of our life here, and someday when I am not so busy, I will write more, so our children will have a more detailed account of this home we all love so much.

I snuggled down into bed, put a pillow over my head and dropped off to sleep. Dreams of Mothers experiences in the book she wrote remained in my mind. The part about the wind, and Mother's feelings she so aptly put into words was very meaningful, as I too was often lulled to sleep by the whispering of the wind.

These are my Mother's feelings about the wind as she wrote in her book about the homesteading life of she and my father.

"The wind begins to blow ferociously, bending the limbs of trees until they almost touch the ground. I love the wind. To me the wind is exciting, awesome, and mysterious. I wonder if God is speaking to me; reminding me, yes, the whole world exactly who really is in charge of this big wonderful universe he created. The wind is soothing to my soul. I feel the presence of God and know that his omnipotence is everywhere. Many people hate the wind. They find the roar and strength unbearable. Not me! I enjoy the whistling, roaring sound it makes as it blows threw the trees. Call me crazy if you wish, but that doesn't change the way I feel. Maybe I am a bit different, and strike some people as being in between eccentric and sage. I do not apologize, because I am happy being that way. The wind is still blowing, and I am being lulled to sleep by the relaxing sound of the wind." I closed the book and knew my mother really did need to add more experiences of those days so long ago.

I marveled at the stamina my parents had shown during those difficult years. Sometimes I have doubts as to how much of their determination and desire to be successful has been handed down to me. The years ahead will tell the story!

Chapter 3
THE STORM

AFTER READING the story my mother had written about her homesteading days, I now knew why my parents had made the decision to come to Wyoming. I felt very relaxed and dropped off into a deep sleep.

Suddenly I was awakened by the loud clashing of thunder and streaks of lightening flashed through my window until it lit up the whole room. I lay in bed listening to the loud sounds of thunder and lightening, wishing it would stop so I could get back to sleep, but it only became louder and more fierce sounding. I remembered something I had heard my father say; when thunder comes shortly after flashes of lightening, it means the lightening is very close. This saying really did not mean much to me, as I was usually tucked safely under my bed covers and felt safe from the outside storms. I knew from living in Wyoming almost my entire life that storms like this one were a regular happening, but possibly because I was older now and realized the danger of these storms, I had begun to worry a bit when the wind started to blow. I went to the window and could see trees blowing with their limbs almost touching the ground. This was not a good sign. About the same time I looked out and saw the tree limbs bending down, I heard the voices of my parents. They were up, peering out the window between flashes of lightening trying to see if the barn door had blown open, and if any animals were out running around in this storm. Before I could join them in the living room we heard a deafening clash of thunder. I ran to the front room; still in my pajamas, when my father shouted. "It has hit the barn, the barn is on fire! Mother ran to her bedroom, grabbed a robe, and a pair of pants, threw them in my father's direction and they were out the door, with my father still struggling to get his pants on while running out the door. They were gone in less than five seconds. I also grabbed some pants and was out the door, just in time to jump into the back of the truck, headed for the barn. The barn was a little less than a quarter mile from our house. We knew we could not put the fire out, but maybe we would get to the barn soon enough to save the baby calves and hopefully their mothers. Calving season was in full swing, and due to the cold April weather we kept the cows that were near calving in the warm barn.

Our community was twenty miles from a fire station, so we knew our barn would be burned to the ground before firefighters could be there. We had a fire hydrant for watering the stock near the barn. We quickly hooked up the hose and my mother began spraying water while father and I ran into the barn to try to herd the cattle out to safety. Smoke was everywhere, which made breathing difficult. Some calves were too young to guide out and we picked them up and carried them outside and away from the burning barn. When I returned from a trip with a baby calf, I heard my mother screaming something about father. I knew I had not seen him for a couple of minutes and felt an overwhelming fear that something was terribly wrong. The barn was dark except for some flashes of lightening. Smoke was now heavy and black all through the barn. I started looking and saw that my dad had gone back to a dark corner to save a baby calf. He had tripped over a bale of hay and fell. I did not see him move and the calf was running loose, so I figured the worst had happened. Dad had been overcome with smoke after he had fallen. I screamed at the top of my lungs to my mother for help, but with the wind blowing and cattle bawling, it was impossible for her to hear my calls for help. My father was a large man and I knew I was not strong enough to get him out of the burning barn alone. Luckily, when mother realized that I was still in the barn, she dropped the water hose, and ran into the barn. she heard me yelling "Mom back here." She was near enough by now to hear my voice and came to my aid. We dragged my father outside to safety. Although I had paid little attention to the CPR lessons I had taken in Agriculture class, I would try anything to save my Dad. While I clumsily administered CPR, mother was applying water to father's face. What a relief, when he finally showed signs of consciousness we both sighed a breath of relief. In a few minutes he seemed to be back to normal and in charge of the situation again. The word soon spread around the community that mother and I had saved father's life. Mom and I had swelled heads as big as a couple of huge watermelons. When it was all over, we were very thankful that we had not lost any of our cows or calves. We erected a make-shift barn to use until fall, when we harvested crops and could afford to build a much nicer new barn.

Chapter 4
MISSOULA

CARLA AND I hadn't talked since she left for college, and I really felt like telling her about the barn fire and how Sapphire and Harmony were doing. I knew that her parents were in touch with her on a regular basis, and when I asked them how she was doing they always seemed willing to talk about her. I knew she liked college very much and in a way I envied her getting to go away to school, but there were many reasons that I decided to go to our local Junior College. I was satisfied with my classes and had made a few new friends from towns around the area. I was satisfied with my life, but missed Carla very much. Carla was living in a Sorority Dorm, and from conversations with her parents they had mentioned that the rooms were very small and she was unhappy living in such crowded quarters, and that when this year was over, she would be able to take a place off campus. Freshmen attending

college and are away from home are required to live in
dormitories one year and then they are allowed to live
off campus.

When the phone rang, instead of Carla's voice I
heard, it was her room-mate. I asked to speak to Carla,
and` she told me in a matter of fact way that Carla was
out on a date. I don't know why I was so shocked that
she was on a date, but lets face it. I had never thought
about our friendship in a way that would bring out the
kind of jealously that I suddenly felt when I heard that
my Carla would be dating someone else. True, we were
friends, in fact the best of friends. We talked, danced,
went to ball .games, horse-races; in fact neither of us
had ever talked about or cared about dating anyone
else. So when this pang of jealously came over me, I
was totally unprepared for such feelings. I hung up
the receiver, and began cramming for a test that was
scheduled for the following Monday. I could not keep
my mind on the material I was working on. Regardless
of how hard I tried, my mind went back to Carla and
her date. I wondered what this guy looked like. What
was there about this guy that led Carla to go out with
him? I knew I was being silly and acting like a baby
over a toy, but I could not get rid of those thoughts. I
turned the radio on, thinking perhaps music would ease
my mind. I went to bed, with the music blaring, and
finally dropped off into a restless sleep. I slept a while
and dreamed a while; often about outlandish things.
As usual, when morning came my mind had calmed
down and I was able to go about my chores in the usual

way. I made the decision to have a talk with Carla, even if I had to drive all the way to Missoula, Montana to do it!

At breakfast we were having a family discussion about a variety of things. Of course the new barn we planned to build took priority. A new barn was going to be costly; financing for it might be a problem, as we planned to build a much larger barn than the old one, and perhaps add a few extra features our old barn didn't have. When the barn discussion died down, I asked if either Mom or Dad knew how far Missoula, Montana was. I realized I was now a freshman in college and had never taken a trip alone. Sure, I had been on a few family vacations; traveled to places, like California and New York, but always with my parents. I figured I was ready to get out on my own and be independent. Missoula would be a perfect start. I told my parents about the trip, and they agreed that visiting Carla would be a nice thing to do, not knowing I had a more personal reason for seeing her. They knew I missed talking to her, so were pleased for me to see her. I visited Harmony and Sapphire, so I could give Carla the latest news about her horses, and told her parents I was going to Missoula to visit Carla. Carla's mother, without hesitation, asked if I would mind delivering a package to her. She handed me a wrapped box and explained that she really did not want to send it by postal mail. They wished me a good trip and I promised to see them when I returned home on Sunday afternoon.

I worked steadily on my assignments the following week, so I would not get behind in my studies. I was assigned a ten page essay to write on "Why I chose to become a farmer." Writing Essay's was not an easy thing for me to do, but I finished it by Friday. Now I could relax and enjoy my trip. Saturday morning arrived, and I was on my way. It took about five hours for me to make the drive. I found myself in Missoula; Now, the next thing was finding the college. My visit was going to be a surprise for Carla, so I didn't call her for directions. I asked at a service station and with the kind attendant's help I was on my way again. It was about noon Saturday morning when I finally reached the dorm where Carla lived. I knew I would not be allowed to go to her room, so I asked the receptionist to call Carla and tell her she had a guest downstairs. I didn't give my name, and was hoping she was home and would come down to see who her guest was. The receptionist said that Carla would be down soon. I was very nervous, because I had no idea how our meeting would be. Was she dating someone she cared a lot for or was last Friday nights date only a casual thing.

I was sitting on a couch with my back to the stairs, expecting to wait a few minutes until she came down, then I heard her yell, "Mark, Mark! I can't believe you're here. She ran to me, gave me a big hug, all the time squealing, you're here, you're here!" Of course I returned the hug and said, "Lets go outside where you can make all the noise you want to." I held her hand and we walked outside. Those hugs were the first time we had come anywhere near showing that much affection.

I was really happy for such a great greeting. I no longer felt jealous. I led her to my car and we began talking about everything that had happened since she left for school. I told her about my classes, about Sapphire and Harmony, and of course about the barn fire. We were just beginning to get caught up, and I suddenly realized two hours had passed and we were only beginning.

Carla and I had been so interested in our visiting that I had forgotten to give her the package from her mother. I reached into the back seat and handed her the package from her mother. She knew immediately her parents reason for sending the package. Monday was her birthday! Oops, I had made another boo-boo. I had forgotten her Birthday! Carla ripped the brown wrapping off and opened a beautifully wrapped package. "Come on," I said, "Quit stalling, I want to see what I hauled all the way from home to Missoula." When she finally very carefully opened her gift, it was a beautiful watch with her name engraved on the back. She didn't hide her surprise, simply did her squealing as she had done when she discovered me at the dorm.

At the very end of school, Carla left her watch in her locker while she was in gym class, and it had been stolen. Her parents felt she had been much too careless and were in no hurry to buy a new one. Besides her old watch was not a nice one and she'd had it all through high school .

Since I did not have a gift for her, I asked her to dinner as my birthday gift to her. She accepted and we were on our way. After dinner, I decided to find a motel room where I could spend the night, hopefully somewhere near the college. Carla knew the perfect place, as she and her parents stayed there when they brought her to Missoula to enroll in college.

My trip to Montana ended much too soon and It was time for the long drive home. I think both of us knew, a kiss was long overdue. It wasn't a passionate kiss, but a warm and much more affectionate kiss than I ever expected it to be. I was very happy about my trip to Missoula, but was eager to get the drive over. It was a long drive and I knew I needed to get home and help my Dad with the chores he had been doing for me during my absence. Since Montana did not have a speed limit, I was traveling about seventy miles per hour. I had been following a car for quite some time, because the driver was also traveling seventy, and I did not feel safe passing her on this busy highway. Suddenly she slammed on her brakes to keep from hitting a deer that was crossing the road in front of her car. She could not avoid the deer, and hit it. A few miles back I had noticed a sign that said, "Watch for Deer Crossing." These signs are prevalent in Montana due to the heavy population of deer in that state. When she hit the deer, she also lost control of her car, over-corrected and rolled over several times. By the time I could get away from traffic and get parked I dashed to her car. It was already in flames. She had miraculously been able to crawl out of the car, and was yelling! "My baby, get my baby out!" I ran to the car. I could see the child on the back seat, but when I attempted to open the door, it was stuck so tightly I was unable to get it open. I tried the door on the other side. The same thing. A trucker had seen me running towards the wreck, and was on his radio immediately calling for help. All the while I was still doing everything in my power to get into the car and save the baby. Just when I was feeling totally helpless, the trucker grabbed a large fire extinguisher and was coming toward the wrecked car. I yelled to him about the baby. He hurried to the car, broke a window and began using his fire extinguisher. Luckily I heard the sirens of a fire truck followed by an ambulance. By using the proper tools, the baby was rescued; seemingly unharmed and unaware of her close call with certain death. When I looked back to where the mother was standing, I saw her lying on the ground. She had fainted. I started CPR and in seconds she also regained consciousness. Both baby and mother were placed in the ambulance, headed for the nearest hospital. As for me, I was so exhausted I sat in my car about thirty minutes before I stopped shaking and was able to continue on my way home. A picture of that baby in the back seat and the helplessness I felt stayed in my mind for days.

Chapter 5
SAPPHIRE AND HARMONY

I REALIZED AFTER I settled down from my visit with Carla in Missoula that too much time had passed and I should be training Sapphire for the up-coming race at the county fair. This was an important race and I knew I should have been training Sapphire much sooner and more intensely. If I could bring Sapphire to my own home it would be much easier to train her. She had raced before and actually at one time beat Nochi in a race. I knew she was a good runner, but needed months of practice. The track where I had trained my beloved Nochi was empty now, so I could use it for training Sapphire. When I visited Carla's parents, I approached them with the idea of moving Sapphire to my place, which was much more suited to training a horse than the crowded lot where Carla's Sapphire and her colt Harmony lived. They agreed that my idea was a good one and realized that since my Nochi died, I probably needed horses around, and also Sapphire could be properly trained. I began making plans to bring Sapphire and Harmony to my home. I had Nochi's trailer to use for the transportation, but needed to decide where I would put Sapphire and Harmony to protect them from the storms and bad weather that hit Wyoming often. We needed a place for those horses to be out of the weather. I told my father that I wanted to bring Sapphire and Harmony to our place, so I could train them and that the arrangement was agreeable with Carla's family. My father knew that in my heart I was still missing Nochi so the idea of having horses around appealed to him. The thing I admired most about my Dad was his thoughtfulness. If either of my parents thought I needed or wanted something, they did their best to help out. This time was no different. Father scratched his head in serious thought, and actually came up with an idea that solved the problem. We would erect a temporary shed near the riding arena where I had spent so many hours training Nochi. It was a perfect idea. We figured out how much lumber it would take to build a small shed and my father was ready to buy new lumber, when I suggested we take a look at our burned barn and see if we could salvage enough material for the shed. Both of us were pleased and surprised that some lumber had survived the fire and was just laying there ready to be used.

When my classes for the week were over, we worked at building our shed. The week-end found us sawing, and nailing boards and by Sunday evening we had a new shed for Sapphire and Harmony. I needed help loading the horses into the trailer, so I ask my sister Kati if she would come along. Kati and I were good pals in past years, but since I was in college and she was a Sophomore in high school we had not spent much time together. In my mind, Kati was still a baby and we had nothing in common. Kati was into "keeping up with the crowd" which left her very little time for family. She actually was a good looking little chick, with her red hair, blue eyes and creamy complexion. Even though I admired her looks, there were times when she acted her age. Most of the time clothes and parties were all that seemed to matter. I told my parents how I felt, which only caused trouble between us. Kati loved horses, so I knew she would be happy to help me bring them home. Also Carla and Kati liked one another and I figured Carla would be happy for Kati to ride her horse. Also when I was training Sapphire I needed someone to time her speed, so I could ride her, and know how much progress she was making from day to day.

Carla's parents said their good-byes to Sapphire and Harmony, then Kati and I headed for the ranch. I was happy that Kati actually would take time off from her boy friends and other social activities to help train Sapphire. Of course we spent some time with Harmony, even though we were not actually training her for riding yet. When we unloaded our guests, they showed us how much they enjoyed their new surroundings by kicking up their heels, and running around like two children playing in a park!

College was hard for me. I figured being raised on a ranch, agriculture would be a snap. Wrong! There were so many things about ranching and farming I had never dreamed of that I found myself in a quandary much of the time. Life was very busy. I needed to spend more time on my school work, and less time training Sapphire.

I was assigned to write a ten page essay in English. English was a required class which I desperately wanted to get out of the way, so the essay was important toward my future graduation. I chose to write the essay about horses. My own experience with horses, things my mother and father told me and, material from the Library gave me plenty of information to write about. I had read and seen movies about how Indians broke or tamed wild horses they found on the prairie. My essay had to be factual, so here is the way they did it. The story sounds unbelievable, but is very true. After teaching a horse to be led with a rope on its neck they took it to the creek, got on its back and tried to ride. Of course the horse kicked and bucked so much the Indian fell off, but the rider was not injured because he was in the water. The horse could not run away, so the rider simply got back on and tried to stay on again and again until at last the horse settled down and there-after was willing to be ridden. A few anecdotes like this one and I would have my essay written. Of course since I had not taken typing in high school I had to use the old find and pick system to get it typed, and that would be very slow.

Carla warned me in high school that I needed to take typing and now I wish I had followed her advice.

In our family, we had a custom of everyone getting to the table for breakfast on Sunday mornings. We discussed all family matters; things that happened to each of us. Good or bad we were encouraged to share with the family. My mother served hot-cakes and those hot-cakes alone caused us to show up no later than nine o'clock for the family get-together. Of course, this morning the main subject centered around our two additions, Sapphire and Harmony. Katie couldn't wait to find out when we could start teaching Harmony to be ridden. She was almost two years old now and it was time to teach her to wear a saddle and carry a rider. Kati was determined to be Harmony's first passenger! I had not planned to put a saddle on Harmony until the big race was over, but Kati insisted . She kept her promise to help, so both of us began the big project of training Harmony, and getting Sapphire ready for the race.

Many days were too cold, or I needed to study, but by spring Harmony wore a saddle and Sapphire was gaining speed. Carla was surprised and happy with the progress we had made with her horses when she came home for a short Thanksgiving holiday. I was looking forward to the end of the semester when Carla would be home for the summer and could take over much of Sapphire's training. Spring and summer meant helping my Dad with the many new chores that come to farmers at that busy time. I needed to be in the field running machinery, or doing what ever my father called on me to do.

As I carefully drove our large John Deere tractor down the rows of corn cultivating to cut out the many weeds that sprang up amid the rows, I stopped as I often did to rest my eyes from the grueling job of keeping my eyes constantly on the rows; making sure I didn't swerve a bit and cut the corn plants along with weeds.

Heart Mountain stood tall and majestic in the not too far distance. I never tire of looking at the mountain as it was a sight that never seemed to escape my eyes. A person looking in that direction could not help but wonder how it came to be called Heart Mountain. It certainly is not heart-shaped like we use as a symbol of a heart, like we see on a Valentine or box of candy. It has its own shape which is nothing like the symbol we use. There is a tale handed down by the Crow Indians of long ago that claimed the mountain was shaped like a human heart. So it has always been called, "Heart Mountain." Perhaps, by using a persons imagination, it could actually resemble the heart of a human or animal. Surrounded by sagebrush, it stands alone, with its unusual limestone cap, Heart Mountain is a puzzle. Geologists from around he world have studied it, yet it remains a passionate debate.

Heart Mountain is also used by the locals as a weather predictor. When clouds hang over the mountain, we see rain, hail or even a snow storm coming to our valley. Today when I looked at Heart Mountain, I saw clouds. They hovered in the sky just above the mountain and

I decided to keep an eye them. After I had driven the tractor up and down several rows, I stopped again and glanced at the mountain and the sky around. As I suspected, clouds were moving in. I thought of rain, which was something farmers really needed, because of no rain during the summer months. It might also be snow, but it's a little early for a snow storm. I vowed to keep an eye open for whatever old man weather had in mind. One thing I was certain that those clouds looked ominous. I stayed with my tractor work until one field was finished, but because the wind was beginning to blow, I decided to wait until morning to do the other field.

The wind was blowing very hard now, so I went directly to the corral to take care of the animals. I noticed that Harmony was not in the corral nor the shed which was a bit strange, but as unpredictable as my sister Kati was, I figured she had taken Harmony for a ride. True, it was late for a ride and especially to go up in the hills. She must have gone further than the route we normally took. I was a bit worried, but Kati was an excellent rider and I trusted her completely. She would no doubt be back before the rain started. By this time, the wind was strong, and sprinkles were falling.

"Why didn't I listen to the weather forecast this morning on the radio? Why did I ride so far?" Kati mumbled to herself. Mark warned me about riding too far alone. I should have listened to my brother. It will be dark in a short time, and I am afraid I won't get back to the coral with the rain coming down and wind blowing, It will take me longer to get back. I'll go as fast as I can, maybe Harmony will cooperate. I have never pushed her into a gallop, I don't know how she will handle going that fast. I guess I will walk her fast and maybe trot a little. I can hear Mark saying, "Kati do not push her, she hasn't been wearing a saddle very long, and we don't want to make her nervous."

I hate to admit it, but my brother is usually right about things, especially horses. The wind is blowing harder now, and Harmony doesn't like it. She veers in the direction the wind is blowing, making it very difficult for me to keep her on the path. We are getting soaked from the rain. I should have brought an umbrella. I guess that doesn't make since because reining the horse and holding the umbrella would be almost impossible. I guess I will keep going until I find a tree to get under for protection. It is pouring rain now, so that I can hardly see where I am going. I hope Harmony will follow her instincts and stay on the trail. Suddenly I felt something hitting me in the face. I looked down and it was hail! Not large hail, but it was falling fast. The balls of hail were getting larger and more rapid, falling wth a force such as I had never seen before. Harmony and I were traveling against the wind. Hail Stones were beating my face and body like golf balls. Harmony was getting the same pounding as I. Hailstones were getting larger by the minute. Harmony was out of control. I dropped the reins, to protect my body. She was kicking her back legs, running around in a circle. Her whirling around caused me to slide off, landing on the ground which was covered with hailstones as large as golf balls. I bumped my head when I fell, then suddenly began to feel dizzy. Another time in my life I fainted after taking a serious fall, so I knew I was beginning to loose consciousness. Of course at this point I didn't realize that the hail had stopped as suddenly as it started or that my family were desperate to find me.

When the rain first started, Mark looked in the coral and the temporary shed we had built for Sapphire and Harmony. Sapphire was there, but Harmony was nowhere to be seen. He rushed to the house and reported to Mom that Kati was missing. Of course she went into hysterics, Crying, "Lets find her, hurry! my baby, my baby, lets go. Mark, I will get some umbrellas and coats while you bring the truck around. We can leave your father a note, so he will know where we are." She scribbled a few words to Dad, and we took off. The hail had stopped but the rain was pouring down, which made driving more hazardous. I thought I knew the direction Kati had gone, so we headed in that direction. Kati loved to ride in the hills. The road was narrow and rough, so traveling was slow.

About two miles, down the road we sighted her. Lying in the middle of the trail, with her face between her arms as if she thought the hailstones were still beating her face and body. Mom and I rushed to her, holding our breath, hoping she was still alive. When Mom called her name she moved her arms, raised her head slightly and stared at us. She had gained consciousness, but was still in a state of shock. We didn't try to talk to her; just carried her to the truck. When she was safely seated in the truck, out of the wind and rain, she opened her eyes. Mother wrapped her in a warm dry coat which didn't help much as her clothes were soaked. Her first words were, "Where is Harmony? I think she ran away. I think I lost Harmony. Please find Harmony!'

I wanted to find Harmony just as badly as Kati did, or more so because I could not imagine having to tell Carla that Harmony was gone. We took Kati home as fast as we could travel on the narrow muddy trail. Mother was trying to consol Kati, and keep her warm, which was actually impossible with her soaking wet clothes and bruises on her arms and face where the hailstones had beat down on her. By the time we arrived home the rain had stopped, although the wind was still blowing hard. My Dad was standing in the front of the house trying to figure

out what was going on with his family. I honked the horn long and loud, to let Dad know something was very wrong. He came to the truck and carried Kati into the house with Mother following close behind. Mother said, "Go with Mark, he needs you. I will take care of Kati."

We knew Harmony could have run any direction. When we reached the prairie, we drove slowly hoping to catch a glimpse of her somewhere. When we reached the place where we had found Kati, I stopped the truck and each of us started in different directions, trying to find hoof tracks on the wet ground. Sure enough my father gave a loud whistle. I headed in his direction.

There were horse hoof tracks leading toward a reservoir where irrigation water is stored until needed by people when watering crops. She was standing near a cabin that had been built many years ago for use by workers when they were building the reservoir. In her effort to outrun the hailstorm she had come to the end of the prairie, where more farms were located. Probably a distance of at least five miles. After much effort, we were able to get close enough to pick up the reins. My father walked to the truck and I rode Harmony back home and into the coral. What a relief we felt to have found our horse. The possibilities of her demise were many. She could have fallen and broken a leg or she could have kept going to a road where some person who wanted a horse kept her for their own. My imagination goes wild when I think of how dangerous it is for a lost horse. When we reached the coral, darkness had fallen, but she kicked up her heels and, whinnied as if to show me how happy she was to be home again.

When I walked into the house, I could sense that things were not normal. My parents were not bustling around getting ready for dinner as usual. I knew immediately that I would find them up in Kati's room. When I stepped in the door, Mother looked at me and shook her head. Katie was in her pajamas and robe, lying on the bed. She appeared to be sleeping. I thought when I saw her sleeping that she was only resting from her bad experience in the hailstorm, until I realized she was not in a normal sleep. My father said, "We are taking your sister to the hospital. Seems like when she fell she hit hard on a rock or perhaps a hailstone. Looks like something very bad is wrong. We called Dr.Katenhorn and he thinks it best to bring her in to the hospital, where he can do an xray and observe her carefully for a day or so. I will stay until the examination is over and we have the results, then I will come back here. Your mother will stay with her." Don't worry about things here, Dad, I will take care of everything." I assured him, but at the same time, I dreaded taking on the responsibility. What if one of the cows needed help with birthing a calf? Certainly I had helped my Dad with this kind of thing for years, but my father always used his expertise, and I was only the helper. This would be my first experience, and needless to say I felt a big load on my shoulders. Dad reassured me that I would be fine; that he trusted me completely. I also knew that if Kati's reports were not good, I might have to run this farm all by myself for several days. "Good luck, Mark" I told my self, and I said a little prayer that things would work out okay. I finished feeding and watering the animals, checked all the gates to be sure none of the animals would get out, visited Sapphire and Harmony, as I did every night before heading home.

Chapter 6
KATI

IT WAS very late, probably around eleven p.m. I was cramming for an exam that was scheduled for the next day, when the phone rang. It was my father with news about Kati's condition. His voice did not sound as cheerful as it usually did. "Mark," he said. "I'm sorry, but I have a very upsetting report on Kati. the Dr. did an x-ray of her head and found an aneurysm very close to the brain. We are taking her to Billings for more tests. She is sleeping or in a coma much of the time, so we will take her in an ambulance. If you are like I was, the word aneurysm is absolutely foreign to you. The Doctor explained, as best he could in words that your mother and I could understand. It is a growth formed by an enlargement in a weakened wall of an Artery. It could be in a vein, heart, or even the brain. He stopped talking for a short time; then continued. "Mark, aneurysms are very dangerous, so Kati will need all our help and prayers to survive this.

Your Mother will go with Kati in the ambulance, and I will drive to Billings. Be brave, Mark, and I will be calling every day to see how things are going. Also, I may be able to get home in a couple of days." "Hey, Dad, don't hang up yet! How did this happen?" I had an idea, but wanted to hear it from him. "Son,we may never know for sure, but I'm thinking when Kati passed out and fell from Harmony, she hit the ground falling on one of those large hailstones that were beating her on the head, or on a rock so hard that it caused all this. At any rate an aneurysm in the brain is very serious. Or there is a remote possibility that the Aneurysm was already starting to grow and the fall or hail triggered the bleeding." "Okay Dad, I had the same idea, but wanted to hear it from you. Thanks for the call and I will look forward to hearing some more later." I hung the receiver up and fell to my knees and prayed for my kid sister.

The semester was coming to an end. I worked hard on my school work and passed all my classes. No A's, just B's and C's. Even though my grades dropped a bit after Kati's accident, I had managed to keep my mind on school. It was not an easy thing to do, with many extra farm chores, and since my Mom was still at the hospital with Kati, I was in charge of the cooking and cleaning. My father was home one day and then back to the hospital in Billings, Montana the next. From our ranch to Billings was almost one hundred miles, so my Dad was always tired from the trip, and the many jobs he felt he needed to take care of at home. Kati was still in a coma, and my Mother was staying by her side.

We were anxiously waiting to hear the results of the tests that had been taken. When my father came home I asked him what a coma was as compared to simply being asleep. The Dr. explained it to my parents like this. A coma can be difficult to understand especially when people often jokingly use the words coma, or comatose to describe people who aren't paying attention or who are drowsy or act sleepy, but, a coma is a serious condition that has nothing to do with sleep. If someone is in a coma, he is unconscious and will not respond to voices or sounds or any sort of activity going on around them. You can't shake and wake a person who is in a coma like you can someone who has just fallen asleep. The Dr. went on to explain to my parents that it can be very upsetting and frustrating for a person's family to see someone they love in a coma. After my talk with Father I understood why Mother was staying close by her side because the fact is; Kati might wake up anytime and my Mother wanted to be there when she did awaken.

Two more weeks, and Carla would be home for Christmas. I hardly had time to think about Carla. I tried to call her a couple to times, but she was out. Her roommate answered and said she was in the Library one time, the other time there was no answer, so I decided to simply write a short note with the news about Kati. I trusted her to call me back when she received the note, telling her about my sisters accident. I really didn't have time to wait around for a call that may or may not come. My classes would be over in another ten days, then I would have more free time.

Chapter 7
BILLY THE BULLY

SINCE I was in town at school every day, the job of picking up whatever groceries we needed from the store was left to me. Because my Father and I had lost our cook, we were eating more prepared frozen food these days. Things like T.V. dinners, pot pies and the list went on and on. My Dad certainly was not a cook and although I often helped Mom in the kitchen, my cooking left something to be desired. Both Father and I accepted the prepared food without grumbling about it. We did look forward, however to the day Mother was back cooking our usual wonderful foods. One day while I was shopping, I heard my name; "Mark, hey Mark," I looked around and there was,"Billy the Bully," as he was known when we were in High School. He was into horse racing, as Carla and I were. He owned a good race horse that, I have to admit was a challenge in the races. Several times his horse won over mine and Carla's, and he never let us forget it . Of course, we didn't call him "Billy the Bully" to his face, but he earned that disgusting title by his many accusations and threats. I hoped Billy had changed with a little maturity. I spoke to him in a friendly way, as a friend rather than a foe. But I soon found that he was the same bully as he always was. His first words were, "Well Mark, my man, how is life treating you farmer boy? And that little chic you hung out with. What was her name, Carla?" I ignored his nasty attitude and spoke to him in a civil manner. "Carla's doing great. She is attending college at Montana State University. Doing great!" "Yeah," he said," I heard she went away to some fancy college. I had her pegged as a snob when we were in school. She was so proud of that horse of hers. What was it's name anyhow? Oh yeah, now I remember; something like, Sage or Saggy?" "No Billy Boy, her horse is named Sapphire, and she is going to win the big one this year . I'm sure you are looking forward to the big day!" Billy bristled at the positive attitude I took; just maybe he would lose a race. Billy responded with, "Well I gotta git. I'm chief cook and bottle washer at the new A&W place that just opened up in town." I decided not to go to college, at least this year. I may go in to some kind of business, maybe a Casino!! See Ya!" I was glad to see him go, but knew I hadn't seen the last of him.

My feeling about Billy was right. After I ran into him in the store, it seemed like he was everywhere I went. Every time I spoke or waved to him he mentioned the race that was coming up July 4th at the County

Fair. I never told him that Nochi died or that I was half owner of Carla's horse Sapphires Colt, "Harmony." Or that I was training Sapphire during the time Carla was away at school. I figured the less he knew about our horses the better. In a way, Billy's antagonizing remarks spurred me into action. After Kati's accident, I admitted to myself that I had neglected working with Sapphire, and that I better make time to exercise her and get her in shape for serious training. I was hoping that Kati would be well soon and could help me with the timing and grooming and the many other things required to get a race horse ready to run.

Carla would be coming home for the Christmas holidays in about two weeks. I was looking forward to her being here to do much of the work that had been my responsibility for so long, and besides we could be together again. I dreamed about having long conversations; exchanging talk about college life, plans for next semester and maybe just some "chit-chat" too. I would not be a normal guy if I didn't think about serious dating. I really had no idea what her feelings were in that department. I knew what I was hoping for, but Carla might not agree with my thinking. I guess patience and common sense will give us the answer, but now I need to put the reins on Sapphire and go for a ride!

Things were at a standstill in the hospital where Kati was lying in a coma. Two weeks had passed and no showing of improvement in her condition. Although it was time to get the results of important tests that had been taken about ten days ago. Mother was still by her side, and my father continued to make trips every other day to Billings. It was a busy time on the farm. Of course we had a faithful hardworking hired man to carry on with the work when my father was gone. Even though he had been with us for years, he remained unsure of many things and came to me for answers. He still did not speak or understand English fluently, my father spoke enough Spanish to give him instructions, but I had a problem making him understand my English. I vowed to take a class in Spanish sometime during my time in college. Many extra workers who came to our valley to do farm work were from Mexico, so I knew if I intended to be a proper and successful farmer I would need to speak Spanish. I figured my time in Jr. College would be the time to take Spanish. My classes in a four year college would be more difficult, and I had never been an A student ayway, so I mentally prepared myself for much intense studying.

Riding Sapphire one hour every day gave me time to relax, make plans, or just ponder about life in general. During my hour of riding, I not only thought about my life, but also said a prayer for Kati, dreamed of Carla, and what the future might hold for us. Carla was a very "driven" person. Making good grades, working for scholarships, and keeping up a social life were her goals. On the other hand I was more laid back. True; I aspired to have a college degree, but not to the point of putting my head to the grindstone to attain it. I was happiest when on the farm, playing with my horses, or helping my father, and looking forward to the day I would have my own farm or perhaps being in a partnership with my father.

When Dad pulled into the driveway from Billings, he did not get out of the truck right away as he usually did, but sat there at the wheel with his head down in deep thought. Finally he raised his head, looked at the house as if dreading to come in. I thought he was very tired from the trip, but also had suspicions that he had some other unusual problem; maybe something wrong with the car, but I was totally unprepared for the news he brought. I met him on the porch and ask, "Is something wrong, Dad?" He was slow in speaking, but when he finally said, "Son, yes, I have bad news. Your sister's test results came back today, and they aren't good." Dad had tears in his eyes; something I had never seen before, not even when our barn was gutted by fire. "Son," he spoke hesitantly, "Katie has a Brain Aneurysm. Our doctor thinks we should take her to Mayo Clinic in Rochester. The doctor there will be able to advise us as to further treatment. This doctor at Mayo Clinic is a specialist, with an advanced degree in Neurosurgery. He is a specialist in Cerebral vascular surgery. He is supposed to be the best." I was in such shock I couldn't respond. I put my arms around Dad's shoulders, and said the only thing I could say at this point. "Dad, don't worry, God will not take Kati away from us. She is a tough little gal, she will come through this." I felt a strong urge to protect both Mom and Dad, from their grief, but I knew this thing was pretty much out of our hands. It was up to God now. "When will you be going to this doctor in Rochester?" I asked. "I don't know, son, we have to wait for an appointment, probably be in a couple of weeks."

We walked into the house; I still had my arm around my fathers shoulders. "Sit down Dad, I will see what's in the freezer to eat." We ate our pot pies in silence, both of us deep in thought. I'm sure Father's mind was flooded with memories of better days as was mine.

"You know, Mark, this business of traveling to Minnesota, plus huge doctor bills is taking lots of money." He looked at me, and said, " And I don't know where it's coming from. There was some damage to the crops when we had the hail-storm. Not anything like some of the neighbors had, where it completely destroyed their crops, but enough that our income won't be as much as it has been in years past.

Our family had been so concerned over Kati's accident that we had not discussed how the crops looked after the storm. Sure our crops were not destroyed, as Dad said, but we needed extra, not less this year. I was secretly a bit flattered when my dad spoke about money with me. My parents never talked about money when Kati and I were present. They were careful to keep the subject between the two of them. It was a surprise when he took me into his confidence enough to mention the shortage of money. Of course, at the age of eighteen, I had certainly read between the lines, and realized that there had been times in my life when I had to accept a "Sorry, but no" when I asked to buy something beyond my allowance. I also figured I needed to begin taking part in family finances. So, I felt good when my dad opened up about money, and his problems concerning it. Besides, I would do anything to help get my sister back to her normal life doing all the things she enjoyed so much. Riding horses, swimming, even her social life of dating and giggling with her girl friends over some silly joke between themselves.

Two weeks had gone by with my mother gone. It seemed more like two years. Of course I understood why she stayed at the hospital with Kati; I wouldn't have wanted it any other way, but still I dreaded the emptiness of the house when she was away.

Father stayed home the next day, as was his usual routine, then back to Billings. I am sure he relieved mother from being in the hospital room so much of the time; giving her a chance to relax, and perhaps do a little shopping or simply walk along the streets. Kati was her baby, and she refused to be gone any length of time in case my sister came out of the coma. Two weeks had passed and the coma seemed to be there forever.

It was the sixteenth day since an ambulance pulled out of our driveway for the long ride to Billings. Dad pulled into the driveway, and when he found that I wasn't in the house he immediately headed for the corral. When he drove up to the gate, I had a feeling of overwhelming apprehension. I thought something bad had happened, or just possibly could it be good. I dropped the reins I was putting on Harmony and hurried to the truck. "Dad," I asked, "What's up?" He wasted no time in answering. "Good news, son, Katie woke up today. Not that she is talking, but awake from the coma. The Doctor says, she will be awake for a short time, then drop off into a light sleep; it may be several days, maybe a week before she will be able to stay awake. The news was very encouraging; I was happier than I had felt in almost three weeks. I also knew that the worst was yet to come. I was concerned about the long trip to Mayo Clinic in Rochester MN, and the results of the tests done on Kati's brain aneurysm. The remarks my father had confided to me about the cost of saving the life of my sister, weighed heavily on my mind. It goes without saying that my mother, father, and I would stop at nothing to pay for Kati's return to health.

Two more weeks of school and my first semester of college would be over. I had one more exam to take, so I needed to buckle down and get it right. English was a difficult class for me. Half my grade depended on an essay, which I figured was the part I would spend the most time working on. This was the big one! My chances of passing this test depended heavily on this essay.

I chose to write about my parents early days on the farm and the hardships they endured during the first two years of their homesteading days. The book mother had written served as a basis for the essay, but I would need to add and take away parts of her story. I don't think my professor would appreciate my taking mother's book "word for word." Now if I can just decide on how to get the story started. I would read her story over and perhaps an inspiration of how I wanted to start my essay would suddenly come to me. If my mother was here I could quiz her on things she did not include in her story. But she is not here. She is in Billings, staying beside my seriously ill sister.

'Writing' that is the answer! I will ask her to jot down notes of more favorite memories of the old days. She could do that while sitting hour after hour, hoping a miracle would happen and her "baby" would be well again. I wrote a short letter, asking her to help me out with more favorite things of the early days. I sent the letter along with a couple of good pencils and some paper with my dad to hand to Mom. I knew in my heart that she would do her best to help me with material for the essay. She answered with a note, saying she would have it ready within a week and, Dad would bring it to me. In the meantime I "cooled my heels" and began training Sapphire for the 4th of July Fair Race.

I was in the market buying groceries; trying to find things Dad and I could eat without much cooking, when someone touched my shoulder. I turned and there stood "Billy the Bully." I had not seen him for several days and did not feel like listening to his derogatory remarks about my girl friend or the horses. I decided to be at least civil to him, but the first thing he said was, " Hey farmer boy, looks like you are still hanging out at your same old home pad, running the kitchen for the old man." I was already irritated that he approached me in the store, but his remarks were too much. The last time he called me "farmer boy" I let it go, but this time my temper flared. I raised my arm and hit him squarely in the eye! The minute I hit him, I knew I was in for trouble. He hit me back on my nose. It started bleeding profusely, and I was ready to push him back, when I heard one of the store workers yelling, "Break it up, you guys, stop it! or I'll call 911 for the cops." Billy turned and walked away, and I was left standing near the deli, with my nose still bleeding . A customer who had over heard and witnessed the entire scene was nice enough to hand me a roll of paper towels out of his shopping cart. I thanked him several times, and assured him I would replace the roll of towels he had furnished me. I cleaned my face up in the bathroom, paid for my groceries, found the paper towels, and placed them in the helpful person's shopping cart, then headed for home. I knew I would have to face my father when he returned from his trip to Billings. Never in my life had I hit anyone. I knew the whole thing was my fault, but Billy's nasty remarks triggered an emotion I didn't know I had.

There was no way I could hide my scuffle with Billy from my father, when I had this ugly red swollen nose. I would have to confess to hitting Billy first because of his arrogant attitude, but most of all the name calling. I am very proud to live and work on a farm and plan to do it the rest of my life. The way he spoke the words, "farmer boy" caused me to think that he meant to be degrading to my life style as a farmer. The feeling carried over to my family and our many friends who were also farmers.

Part of me was proud to have defended farmers as a whole, and the other part was ashamed that I lost my temper and started the fight.

"Hey son, what kind of a post did you run into?" My Dad asked jokingly, never dreaming that I actually had been in a fight. "Yeah Dad," I said. "I'll tell you about it later. Let's eat some of this delicious frozen food I have cooked up for us." I tried to be as casual as he had been about my nose. "How are Katie and Mom doing?" "Oh, about the same. No change." he said, obviously wanting to change the subject. "Now, tell me about that nose." Those were the words I dreaded to hear. I knew I had to be honest. I had never lied to my father, but how would I answer that embarrassing question. "Well Dad," I mumbled. "I was in the market shopping on my way home and someone tapped me on the shoulder. It was Billy Henson. You probably remember him. He was always in the 4th of July races; even won over Nochi a couple of times. We called him "Billy the Bully" because that is exactly what he is. A regular bully. Makes all kinds of hateful remarks, pushes people around; stuff like that." My Dad interrupted with, "Okay son, let's get on with it. What happened?" This is it I thought. Time to bite the bullet and confess. "Okay Dad, Billy insulted me and I lost my temper and hit him. I got him right on the eye. Of course that really made him angry and he socked me on the nose." I waited for my Dad to start his speech, but he surprised me and just sat there, with his fork in his hand. He finally said, "So you hit him first?" "I sure did, Dad, his remark about my being a farmer made me lose all the patience I ever had. I am still not sorry, because he had it coming. This isn't the only time he's mouthed off like that." My father was silent for what seemed like ages, while I sat there; my heart beating like I had run a mile race, wondering what he was dreaming up to do to me. Anything he came up with was fine with me. I did what I had wanted to do for years. I socked "Billy the Bully" squarely in the eye, and was sorry I only did it to one eye. Finally my father said, "Now listen son, fighting never pays off. It only gives you a bad reputation. I'm not going to ask what Billy said that set you off to such an extreme that you fought over it, but from now on, keep your head on and never hit first. All through life there will be times when you feel like hitting, but think first! I know this from my own experience when I was a young man. I was young and crazy once myself. But if that nose of yours gets it again I will not be as understanding as I am this time." As usual I listened to his little speech and treasured his words. "I will never fight again!" Kati has been staying awake much more this past week, and the doctor in Billings has agreed that her condition has improved enough that she can come home until her upcoming Mayo Clinic appointment.

My father will bring Kati and Mom home tomorrow. What a great day that will be to have them home. I'm sure Kati will not be riding Sapphire until her aneurism has been treated, but even if she has to be very careful, we welcome her home. As for my mother, well that's even better. No more frozen dinners for Dad and me.

Christmas is only two weeks away and Carla will be home for almost one month. I have missed having her near, more than I will admit to myself or anyone else. Both of us are finishing the first semester of college. Time goes by quickly and one year will soon be over. If Carla chooses not to attend summer school, she will be near enough for us have more long conversations. Yes, I missed her very much!

Chapter 8
LOVE

COULD THESE feelings I have for Carla possible be called love? I often ask myself this question. My needing her in so many ways, and how do I know love when it comes? Is our relationship a deep friendship or could it be more? The fact is, we have never come close to a discussion about our relationship. Carla seems to accept me as a friend only, nor has she given me any reason to think otherwise. She has a social life with her college friends, and even dates occasionally. I am certainly not the only man in her life these days. Common sense tells me to stop this daydreaming and get busy with my chores.

I was in the process of finishing my barnyard chore; locking all gates, making sure all water tanks were filled, and that all the animals were in pens where they should be, when I saw my family turn in the driveway leading to the house. I quickly scanned the barn and corral area, making certain everything was done; hopped in my truck and was there to welcome them. I gave my mother a big hug and even put my arm around Kati, and said, "Welcome back Sis!" I saw the surprise in her face, as she smiled and said, "Me too, Mark, now we can start our ribbing and teasing again. Frankly I missed that stuff." She had no idea how much I had missed our "batting back and forth," We enjoyed Mom's cooking again, along with a lot of conversation about news of neighbors, and their happenings. Kati's upcoming trip to Mayo Clinic was saved for another time.

Katie and Mom had been home almost two weeks, when the doctor in Billings called with the news that Kati's appointment at Mayo Clinic had been confirmed. The date was January 15th. This was about two weeks later than we hoped for, but the specialist was overloaded, and that was the first opening he had. Dr. Wilcox was a famous doctor in his field, and people from the United States as well as other countries came to him for surgeries and other brain conditions. Our doctor in Billings felt lucky to get Kati an appointment as soon as January. Kati was not feeling any pain and seemed to be back to her normal self. She was soon on the phone calling friends, shopping with my mother for Christmas gifts, and even attended a birthday part for one of her "giggly" girl friends. She was home again and in no hurry to get to Mayo Clinic.

My classes ended for the Christmas holidays, and Carla would be home in about three days. Final exams were coming up the week after I returned to end the semester, but I put them out of my mind . I planned to cram the last few days of my vacation, but for now; I would enjoy having Carla back in town. If the weather stayed nice we could work with Sapphire, take in a couple of movies, and most importantly have fun before going back to the rigorous routine.

Carla took a plane from Missoula to Billings, Montana where her parents met her and then home to Powell, Wyoming. Powell is small town of five thousand people, except on Saturdays and Sundays, or special occasions when the surrounding ranchers come in for supplies. We farmers drive over fifteen miles often, for only a quart of milk or loaf of bread. School buses need to travel as far as twenty five miles or more to get children to school. Powell is my town. I attended twelve years of school there and now I am attending a wonderful Junior College there.

When the phone rang last night, I knew it was Carla. I thought the moment it rang, my long wait was over. I heard her voice; the same sweet voice, I had listened to so many times in high school. "Hey kid, I'm back!" she said. I answered with, "Hey kid, I'm glad you're back." We both laughed nervously a bit and then both of us started talking at once. "Go ahead Carla, you first," "No you first, Mark." She said hesitantly. "When are you coming out to visit those horses of yours?" I coaxed. Both of us knew the horses came second to seeing each other. "How about tomorrow morning?" She asked. "Sounds good to me, Carla, so tomorrow it is." I felt light hearted and happy for the first time in months. Kati was home, my mother was home and Carla was home. What more could a guy ask for? The three women in my life were back where they belonged. I went about my chores with a happy heart.

I brushed the horses until their coats, tails and manes were shiny, soft and fluffy.

When Carla pulled in to the barnyard, I wasted no time in dropping the grooming brush and going straight to her car. I greeted her with a big bear hug; not the kiss I had dreamed about. My heart and body certainly felt like it, but something held me back! The time was not right, but I knew somehow, one day or night soon, I would kiss her and when it happened, it would be worth the waiting. Carla was surprised and happy with the way I had cared for the horses. We saddled them and away we went. We rode up the trail where Kati had her accident, and I showed her how far Harmony had gone in the hail-storm. As we rode we exchanged newsy things, like my fight with "Billy the Bully" among other less exciting things. After a couple hours, she looked at her watch and said, "Oops, I need to get started back home," We gave Sapphire and Harmony a nudge in the flanks and headed for the corral. We decided to take in a movie the following night. We waved goodbye, and she was gone.

We spent the holidays much as I hoped for. The weather stayed nice, so we rode horses, went to a Christmas dance sponsored by a young people's group that Carla had been active in many years, and of course saw a couple of movies at the local theater. Carla spent time with her friends; several of which were attending school at the junior college in Powell. The home college is not a shabby school. We have many highly educated professors among the teaching staff who prefer living in a rural area instead of accepting positions in larger colleges. Several of them are avid hunters and fishermen.

Wyoming is famous for it's rugged mountainous areas, that are so appealing to all kinds of summer and winter sportsmen. Graduates who prefer to live at home, or live in nearby towns and find going away too expensive are proud to have a good college near home to attend.

In Carla's case she received a scholarship to Montana State University, and with help from her parents she could attend a four year college. Carla's father was manager of the J.C. Penny store and held that job for as long as I can remember. Carla's grandparents homesteaded many years before my family came, but soon after the time limit was up for homesteading, they sold their land and moved into town. Mr. Nelson, Carla's grandfather, built the only hardware store in town and operated it until his retirement in the early fifties.

After their retirement, they spend much time in southern Texas; away from the cold Wyoming winters. Carla's parents often escaped the cold by visiting her grandparents in the warm climes of Texas. During one of our gab sessions, Carla mentioned to me that her parents would be leaving for their regular winter trip to

Texas after the holidays, and Carla goes back to school. I often wished my parents would take a vacation during the cold weather, but ranchers need to stay close to home to look after the sheep and cattle. Farmers rarely find a time to be away from their cattle and other animals for any length of time. We have a hired man, but after five years, he still needs advise when something unusual occurrs such as a sick cow or even mending a fence.

Kati's birthday was December 4th. She was still in the hospital, so Mom promised her that we would celebrate as soon as we arrived home. The plan suited Kati fine, as she had asked some months earlier if she could have a pajama party with several of her best friends spending the night. It was a big occasion, and both our parents planned activities, food, and transportation for the girls. Since none of the girls were driving yet, they were to meet at a certain place in town and my Dad would pick them up and return them to their parents. The plan worked out as planned, and before I realized what was happening, there were six "giggly" girls running around our home with whatever girls need to keep them happy overnight. Mother prepared a barbeque style supper, which consisted of Baked beans, French Fries and Pizza. A large birthday cake took center place on the table. The girls ate as if they had never seen food before, then it was time for opening gifts and blowing out the fifteen candles.

It was Christmas Eve. My father and I had driven several miles to a densely wooded area to get a ceiling high Scotch pine tree. Mom and Kati decorated it with ornaments, some of which were souvenirs from things we had on our tree, as little kids. My mother was a sentimental person, and clung to memories, as if at any given time they would disappear entirely and never come back. And so it was with our Christmas tree memorabilia. Each treasured ornament was handled with care and placed in a proper place on the tree. In years past, choosing a tree and dragging it out of the woods was a family fun time, but this year we had to be very careful that Kati did not stumble over a fallen tree limb or some other obstacle that might cause a fall, so Mother and Kati stayed home from the outing. The doctor in Billings warned us that if Kati fell and hit her head, it was very dangerous, and could cause the aneurism to burst. Her very life would be on the line if such a thing happened. We watched her closely without being obvious about it.

After attending a Candlelit service at our church, Dad surprised us with, "How does this family feel about Root Beer Floats, or is it too late for treats?" Of course he knew what the reaction would be. Kati and I both chimed in by kidding back. "Don't you dare pass that A&W!"

The evening was late, and all of us were ready for a good nights sleep. Kati and I had already placed our gifts under the tree early in the day, but Mom and Dad had to go to the hiding place for last minute packages, some of which had been purchased in Billings, during the many days they were waiting for Kati to come out of the coma. I could hear them rustling around downstairs getting their surprises under the tree.

"The stockings were hung by the chimney with care in hopes that Saint Nicholas soon would be there."

My parents clung to tradition like flies to a bowl of sugar. My sister and I were treated the same way come Christmas morning as if we were only five years old. Still in our robes, we downed a glass of orange juice, which had been carefully set out for us on a table along with toast and various jellies, and of course a half cup of diluted coffee, although as we grew older we actually could drink regular coffee. After this little banquet, we retired to the living room for opening of gifts. If course we oohed and aahed over how beautiful our ceiling high tree was this special morning; Kati squealed with delight when she saw the large array of gifts stashed under the tree. " How did you guys; meaning (Mom and Dad) do all this behind our backs?" I joined in with, "Yeah, how did you do it?" Of course our parents loved our comments. They brimmed with pride and satisfaction. Unlike our small family, Carla's family included an aunt and uncle and their children and of course her grandparents. She was busy with family several days during Christmas time and we did not get together for over a week. Only ten more days before both of us would be busy with school again. I was invited to her home for a New Year's Eve party and Kati was also invited to a friends to spend New Year's Eve. After some discussion my parents decided to allow Kati to spend the evening with her friends on the condition that we be safely home by twelve thirty. I felt like I was baby sitting, but kept my feelings to myself. The only kiss I would get this time would be a good-bye peck on the cheek. After all, my dreams of a meaningful kiss had flown out the window. Too many people around and besides I had to drive several blocks to pick Kati up and be home by the time my parents had set. Twelve thirty on the nose, and I knew they would either be on the phone, calling or actually driving into town to check on us. That is exactly what happened. Kati and I were driving home; ten minutes after twelve thirty, when an oncoming car dimmed their lights. I recognized my Dad's truck and slowed down. He also slowed down; we each rolled down our windows. I called to him; as if I didn't already know, " Hey Dad, where are you headed this time of night? I didn't think he appreciated any jokes at this point . He answered, "You know very well where I'm headed." He drove to a spot where he could turn around and followed us home. We beat him home and went straight to our rooms. The matter never came up again!

The following day and every day after New Years, Carla came to help me train Sapphire. Usually Kati came to the corral for a chat with Carla, but only for a short time. She grew tired easily and seemed happy to stay in the house with Mother. They watched favorite soap opera's and when the soaps were over, Mother taught

Kati to knit. Often I would find them both in their favorite chairs reading or working a cross word puzzle together. The time for Kati to make the trip to Mayo Clinic to visit Dr. Wilcox was drawing near and we were all under stress as to the results of her visit to the new doctor.

Dad and I finished our jobs around the barnyard and were driving the short distance home, when he turned to me and ask, "Son, did I mention to you about finances for all this extra expense we are having these days?"

"Yes Dad, you did, and I've been thinking about it a lot. So have you come up with anything?" "Well" he hesitated, "Your mother and I talked it over and decided, the only way out of this situation is to sell some cattle." I knew how hard this would be, as he was trying hard to build the herd up, not get rid of them. "Of course the insurance will pay many of the bills, but there will be thousands of dollars for things the insurance doesn't cover." I know this is a surprise to you, but I need your input about the best way to go. Will it be the older cows or the yearlings which will definitely bring the most money. We would be able to sell fewer; helping hang on to more cattle or sell fewer and have more for breeding ." I value your opinion, so what do you think?"

Suddenly I had become a partner in this business. I desperately wanted to help my father with this and other decisions along the way, but doubted my ability to help in such grown- up decisions. But I am an adult; eighteen years, legal age, college student. I am sure this is the way my father sees me; even if I don't feel it myself. "Gee Dad, I appreciate you taking me into your confidence. Yes Sir, I do have a suggestion and that is all it is, a suggestion, but l would say we sell the older cows; the heifers will soon be our breeding stock, and that is the important thing about building up the herd. So I'd say, sell the older ones." "Okay son, my dad spoke with confidence. "The older ones it is; now the next decision is how many? That depends on the price, and how much money we need. I guess we need to hold off, and find out how much the health insurance comes through with."

My father had, at this very moment taken me as a partner in the business! I could not have been more proud. I had pleased my parents and I vowed I would "stick to my guns," to do my very best, so I could always feel as good about myself as I do at this moment!

The wind is blowing so hard I can hardly walk against it. I hope it slows down before Carla comes, since we planned a long ride; the last one before she goes back to school. I figured this was probably our final good bye and I hoped to put my mind at ease about our relationship. Sure, we were and have been great friends two years or more, but I needed to feel more of a commitment. Going steady sounded much better than our special friendship, however I had not used the words, "Going Steady," out loud to anyone, certainly, not to Carla. Although it had been on my mind for months, the proper time never came. I was hoping this final good-bye might be the time I would gain enough courage to actually, "get it out of my system once and for all."

The wind eased enough for us to be outside, so Carla and I decided to go ahead with our ride. We took the usual trail, past some farms and on into the prairie where farms were scarce, and finally to the head of the irrigation canal. We decided to let the horses drink from the canal, and graze on the few spots of green grass that was left from summer, while Carla and I took refuge on the lee side of a shack that was built many years ago for workers to live in while building the canal. We were out of the wind, and the sun took the chill of winter off. In a few days we would again say good-bye, and would not see each other until Easter vacation.

Carla broke the silence with, "So will you be coming to Missoula for a week-end before the holidays?" I wasn't prepared for a question involving the future, and had to think about it until I was able to give her an answer. "You know how it is, Carla. It depends on a lot of things; if I have a Friday off from school, the weather, how Kati's surgery turns out, so the answer is; I would love to see you, you know that, but have to wait before agreeing to come, so I guess we have to leave that decision for later." She was looking down, chewing on a sprig of grass. I knew she was disappointed that she didn't get the answer she hoped for, but I knew in her heart she understood. I felt very vulnerable about the disappointment she felt. I wanted to take her in my arms, and comfort her, and that's what I did. Impulsively I moved closer, took her in my arms and held her. She relaxed her body, and laid her head on my shoulder. Even though I did not kiss her, I certainly felt like it. I wondered if I felt this way toward her for a simple little disappointment, like my coming to see her; how would I feel if she had a really big problem. I took my arms away, held her hands in mine and said,"Hey kid, it is getting late. We'd better grab those horses and start back, but now that we are spitting out questions, I have one for you. We were walking toward Sapphire and Harmony, still holding hands, which made it easier to stop walking, I turned her face toward me. "This is important." I said, obviously stalling for the right words to come. "Carla, we've been friends a long time and judging from the way I feel about you and hopefully you have some feelings for me, I am hoping we can make an agreement or I should call it a commitment. What say you?"

"Mark," she said, still holding my hands, she looked at me before speaking again. "Mark, you are right. I do care for you very much, but, we're both just beginning college, so we have years of education ahead of us, and to swear to a commitment this early in the game does not sound at all reasonable. Either of us may get to know someone we would like to go to a party, study or dance with, and if we are committed, in fact promised to be only with each other, well I just don't think I'm ready for such a promise. And remember, our colleges are quite far apart. We would only have holidays or summers; that 's just not enough. She came back jokingly using my words. What say you?"

I was unable to hide the hurt I felt, and in spite of trying to hide it, my feelings showed. I didn't feel like giving her an answer, even though she stood there waiting for one. I was afraid if I opened my mouth to answer tears would come and I really didn't want that to happen. We walked to the horses, and started home. Neither of us spoke, until Carla pulled Sapphire to a stop, and broke the awful silence. "Mark, I'm truly sorry, but I only spoke the truth. You know me well enough to recognize that I am only being logical. I do care very much for you, but we need to use a lot of common sense about this relationship. Sometime later, in the future, we can make that decision. For now, lets enjoy ourselves, our horses, and all the things that make us happy, Okay?" She put Sapphire to a trot and headed for the corral. Harmony and I soon caught up, and we rode along in silence. By the time we reached the corral, my disappointment had turned to acceptance and a certain appreciation of her reasoning. She was right, and I apologized for reacting in such a peevish way. Thank goodness, we had the discussion and were now back to the special friendship we always enjoyed. My jealously would always exist, because it was part of my personality, but I would never let Carla see it again. We unsaddled the horses, watered and fed them, chatted about the weather and when she would be back to help train Sapphire. As she prepared to drive away, I reached through the window and gave her a casual kiss good-bye and she drove out of the barnyard and was on her way home.

Christmas vacation ended, and now it was time for the old routine to begin. I had chosen subjects for the coming semester that I knew I could pass without a lot of library work. Research in the library often meant I would need to stay at school late or even drive back in at night. I actually planned my classes with Kati's upcoming surgery in mind. I decided to have a little fun this semester, so instead of swimming or some of the other classes offered for P.E. I enrolled in "Square Dancing" I figured I had plenty of exercise, at home, caring for the animals and all the other chores, but Physical Education was required before I could graduate, so Square Dancing took care of that little problem. Besides I'm sure I would see some good looking chicks trying to learn to Square Dance. So what? A little fun in life, is something everybody needs, right?

Both parents would be gone to Rochester with Kati, which would leave me responsible for running the ranch. Of course I had help from Jose, but he needed to be given complete instructions for each days work.

Kati wanted to go by car to Mayo Clinic, but after some deliberation my parents made the final decision. Mother and Kati would go by plane, and my dad would follow in the car. Their reasoning was that even though it would only be a two day trip in the car, the drive would be much too tiring for Kati. She had frequent headaches and tired easily. Also my father felt the need for transportation during thei stay in Rochester was necessary to get to and from the Clinic. Of course there would be taxi's or busses, but having a car at hand was much better.

The family would be leaving in three days. They would drive to Billings, MT. where Mother and Kati would take a plane, and Dad would continue on to Rochester.

Carla returned to College, and my family far away in another state, left me to manage the farm work, do my school work and try to get time for Sapphire and Harmony. I was over-whelmed with responsibility. I am sure some things will not get done, and I'm afraid it will be the riding and training of Sapphire and Harmony.

My parents and Kati drove away an hour ago. I gave my mother a kiss, Kati a big hug, and wished my father good luck on the long drive alone from Billings Mt. to Rochester, MN. Dad and I had done the chores early before they left, which gave me a few minutes before I headed for school. A strong wind was blowing from the north, and the sky was cloudy. We were overdue for a winter storm, but in spite of the cloudiness, and wind, I didn't expect a blizzard to blow in. our storms usually came from the north, from Canada, but this day it blew in from the east, so I put the weather out of my mind.

I attended classes as usual. The professors were not my favorite people, but I adjusted and in my mind I was satisfied, although we were not far enough into the semester to be loaded with assignments that often took me to the library for research. For this I was thankful, as daylight time was very short and I needed to get home to do farm chores before dark.

When I came out of my last class of the day, and headed outside the building to the car, I was surprised to see flakes of snow falling. By the time I reached the car, I knew I should get home and do my farm chores without any delay. No time today for pulling up to the A&W for a root-beer . I 'd better get on the highway and head for home. The wind was blowing hard, and snow was coming down fast.

By the time, I turned off the highway for the five mile drive to the ranch, I turned the windshield wipers on in order to see to drive. Yeah, I had really misjudged the weather this time. I should have looked to Heart Mountain for weather clues, but my family were leaving and I wasn't thinking of weather this morning. We were in for a blizzard. The wind was much colder, and in a matter of minutes, the temperature had dropped to freezing. Not the kind of weather that a person should be outside doing farm chores in. Without going in the house to change my clothes, I went straight to the barn. I pitched hay to a few cows that my dad had separated from the herd, filled the water tanks, and fed Sapphire and Harmony. By the time I checked all gates and barn doors, making sure they were closed, to keep the animals from getting out, and started for the house, the blizzard had definitely gained in strength.

I knew in reason that Mom and Kati were probably in Rochester by this time, which was seven o'clock, but my thoughts about dad and how far on his drive he might be. I looked at a map that showed a time change of one hour between Wyoming and Minnesota, so Dad probably had stopped for the night. He made a promise to me before he left that he would not drive at night. If he kept his word, which I was sure he would, he was resting comfortably in a motel somewhere. And besides I had not heard weather predictions for other states and didn't really know whether the blizzard was only in this area or if it was storming in other places.

My mom had planned ahead and left me plenty of food to eat. The refrigerator was full of food, so I took out my favorite dishes and ate like it was my last meal on earth. I turned the T.V. on, watched the news and weather, then went to my room to study. I had a complete chapter in history to read, plus some math to work on. I would be getting up early, before daylight to do chores, change clothes and be at school for my first class, which started at eight o'clock.

I made Dad promise me before he left that he would not drive at night. If he kept his word, which I was sure he would, he was resting comfortable in a motel. I had not heard a weather prediction for other states, and didn't know whether the blizzard was only in this area, or if it was storming other places.

My mom knew she would not be cooking for a while, and left me plenty of food to eat. The refrigerator was full of food. I took my favorite dishes out and ate like it was my last meal on earth. I turned the T.V. on, watched the news and then went to my room to study. I had a complete chapter in history to read, plus math to work on. I would be getting up early, before daylight to do chores, change clothes and be at school for my first class, which started at eight o'clock.

Before going to bed I looked out the door, hoping the storm had eased off a bit, but instead the wind was still blowing; in fact I could hardly open the door, because of the strength of it, and I was blinded by snow. It was a good night to sleep, but I had other concerns. I had lived in Northern Wyoming all my life, and I knew what the weather could do to a persons plans. I remembered the many blizzards in the past when all activities were brought to a halt. The temperature dropped below freezing, so the best thing to do is simply nothing! Freezing to death happens if people do not take the wind and cold seriously. Often this happens to out of state people who come here to hunt elk or deer. Those "green horns" as we locals call them have no idea how dangerous the winters in Wyoming can be to those who think they can out-do old man winter.

I remember an incident that was close to our family because they were neighbors and friends. It happened about two years ago. These people had a son, Ralph. He was married at a young age to his longtime sweetheart. The weather was extremely cold, probably around minus twenty degrees, but the cold weather did not stop this young couple from visiting a bar about five miles from their home. On the way home and argument ensued, and when it became out of control, the young wife demanded to be let out of the car. Her husband stopped the car, dropped her off and continued home. About and hour later, maybe a little more than and hour, he returned to where she got out of the car, only to find her lying in the snow, facing the opposite direction from their home, frozen to death.

Never-the-less, I climbed into bed and slept like a baby until dawn. When I arose, and looked out the window, the snow had stopped, but during the night the wind had blown it into snowdrifts, some higher than my head. I am close to six feet tall, but felt like a midget compared to those drifts.

Regardless of the cold wind and snowdrifts, I had to go to the corral and take care of the animals, so off I went. Self confident that I could make it fine; after all this was not the first time I had been out in a storm. At least the snow had stopped falling or I should say blowing in my face. Last evening I had used my head and hooked up the motor heater, and my truck started on the first try. I watered and fed the animals feeling fortunate that my dad had plugged the heater in that kept water from freezing, so the animals had plenty of water, although, I did have to carry buckets of water out to the shed for Sapphire and Harmony. I left the shed door open, so they were free to come out into the corral for exercise. I patted them affectionately and promised to see them again this evening, and headed for home. I felt a huge relief after the chores were done, but realized I really needed to wear more clothing when I returned to the corral tonight. My hands, feet and face were so cold I actually had no feeling left in them. The house felt so warm and comfortable, I dreaded going outside and driving to school; knowing there would be snowdrifts in the road. It was seven thirty, the sun had not come through yet, so I knew it was too early for snow-plows to be clearing the road. I drove through several on the way to town, and made it to school on time. Because of the storm some of the classes were small, as many of the students from small towns around did not trust the weather, and stayed home. About three p.m. when I came out of the building, I was surprised to see that snow was falling again and the wind had picked up speed. I hurried down the highway toward home, but when I came to the country road that led to our ranch, I knew another blizzard was in progress, so I tried to drive faster, even though I was facing directly into the storm. Instead of speeding up, the storm was slowing me down. I drove through a couple of drifts, hoping I could make it through what lay ahead. Driving was becoming more hazardous minute by minute. My windshield wipers stopped working, which left me guessing how to stay in the road. Suddenly, the truck stopped. I kept trying to pull through the drift, but I couldn't budge. The wheels spun, which only caused them to go deeper in the snow. The days were short this time of year, and if the weather was cloudy and stormy, dark came as early as four thirty. I had about thirty minutes of good daylight left to get myself out of this mess. I pushed the car door open against the snow, and managed to reach back to the bed of my truck, where I always carried a shovel. By kicking back some snow, and climbing, I finally reached the shovel. I began to shovel snow, but it was a hopeless job, as the wind blew the snow faster than I could shovel it. I climbed back into the warmth of the truck and tried the motor again, only to discover that the battery was getting weak; in fact if I tried turning it on one more time it would be dead. Extreme cold, such as this would cause a battery to run down, unless the motor was kept running. My mistakes were piling up. I should never have left the highway and started out on his lonely, scarcely traveled road. I pulled my coat collar close up around my face and started walking, thinking if I was lucky I might be able to walk the four miles home. Walking four miles in a blizzard is a challenging trip, but I had no alternative. I had a choice of walking or staying with the car, not knowing when help would come. I was out of breath from trying to shovel out of the drift. If I walked fast I would soon be completely exhausted. My heart was beating fast; partly from the fear I felt, and rightly so. I had let myself get into a situation that was actually a matter of life or death. I plodded on, hoping for a lull in the wind, and snow. I prayed to God to give me strength to carry on. When I gained consciousness, someone was shaking me saying, "Mark, wake up, wake up man, you walked too fast and too far in this blizzard." It was our neighbor, Abe. The snow had subsided a bit, and he noticed that neither the outside lights in the corral, or the big yard light at our house had been turned on. He drove down the road, past the corral, and saw me lying in the road. Not being able to see the turnoff that led home, and because of a high drift, and the blowing snow, I walked or staggered on past the driveway. I made it halfway between our house and the corral. Abe removed my boots, massaged my feet and hands to bring back the circulation; Had he not come, I most certainly would have frozen to death before snow-plows came the next morning. Abe helped me to his car, took me home, made sure our house was warm, and cautioned me not to try doing my chores. He offered to stop by the corral and turn the water on for the stock. I appreciated his help so much, but had to ask one more favor. "Thank you, thank you so much, Abe for rescuing me. One more favor. I have to carry a bucket of water to the little shed beside the corral for Sapphire and Harmony. I will be fine by morning, and can take care of everything." He agreed, and when he turned to leave, I called to him. "Hey Abe, I will never forget this night, and how you saved my life." He waved his hat and left. I decided not to mention about my terrible experience in the blizzard to my father or mother, as it would only cause them to worry about my ability to take care of the farm and myself in a stressful situation. I was very tired and also hungry. I made a sandwich, along with a glass of milk, and went straight to bed. Tomorrow was another day of rising early, taking care of the animals, and getting to classes.

Chapter 9
BILLY THE BULLY

"HEY MARK, how's the farmer boy these days?" I bristled every time "Billy the Bully" called me farmer boy. I am certainly not ashamed of the term farm boy, and if it was anyone besides Billy saying the same thing to me, I would not be bothered by it. Coming from Billy, with his sneer and tone of voice, was a different thing. I had decided to be civil to him, I returned his greeting with,"So what are you up now-a -days, Billy?" "Well farmer boy he retorted, I am waiting to use the gas pump if you stop playing around and get that jalopy of yours filled."

I finished filling my tank, and started inside the station to pay, when he called to me, " Hey man, I'm going to get you for that black eye you gave me in the store the other day." I didn't show him the curtesy of an answer. I climbed back into my car and headed for home. When I stepped inside the back door, I heard the phone ringing. I hurried to answer before the caller hung up. It was my dad calling from Rochester. He asked me how things were going, including our Wyoming weather. I gave him a cheerful reply and then I said, "Dad tell me what I need to hear! What is the news about Kati?" "Oh yes, he said jokingly, I guess you would like to hear about your sister. She made the trip surprisingly well. Didn't get as tired as your mother and I thought she would although, she did experience a couple of fairly bad headaches. We were very impressed with the specialist who is taking care of her. He didn't waste time arranging for the tests to be done. In fact we were able to get the results just this morning. He will begin the pre-op tomorrow and surgery will be the following day. He was very candid with us about the surgery. He wanted us to know that it is a risky operation, and could either be succesful or a failure, but without surgery, the chances for her life were slim. She might live several days, months, or even years, but if the aneurysm burst it would mean sudden death. Naturally, the choice was surgery." My father and mother were totally confident that our Kati, being the fighter she was would survive and be well again. It was in the hands of God and the doctors. The prognosis was so shocking that I could not speak. "Mark. Are you there? Are you on the line?" When I spoke again, my voice was shaky, and my eyes swelled with tears. "Thanks Dad, I will say prayers for Kati. Give mother my love, okay. And say "Hi" to Kati for me Dad." "I'll keep you posted, son." When he hung the receiver up, I said a prayer for my sister. I felt I needed to talk to Carla, so placed a call to her, but there was no answer. I was disappointed, but planned to call again later, after my chores were finished. If there was a person anywhere that would make me feel better, it was Carla.

Darkness was only a few minutes away, and I still had many chores to do. Time passed fast and I had not looked outside, so what a surprise I had when I walked outside. The wind was still blowing, but it was a Chinook wind. This unusually warm wind would soon melt the snowdrifts, and for a very short time bring spring to our valley. People in northern Wyoming loved to have a chinook blow in.

Horses neighed, and kicked their heels up, sheep bleated, and pigs grunted. What a welcome I received when they heard my truck drive into the barnyard. They were hungry animals. The hired man knew nothing about my experience in the blizzard, so he had not fed them. I petted Sapphire and Harmony, and told them why I had neglected them so long. They switched their tails, letting me know they understood. I loved my animals; the reason I chose farming as my life's work.

Classes this semester required more work than before, which meant hours of research in the library. Some assignments were from books that I could check out and take home, but often I used periodicals and encyclopedia's . For this I needed to be in the library so for at least three days each week, I dug into my research, making copies of information I could take home and finish a particular essay or test I was preparing for. I noticed a girl standing behind me like she was waiting to look for a book near where I stood. "Oh, excuse me," I said. "I didn't know you were standing there. Go ahead, I'll finish later." She had a beautiful smile, and said, "Haven't we crossed paths somewhere. In a class perhaps?" When she mentioned class I remembered where I had seen her. She was taking "Square Dancing" for the physical education that was required. She had never been my partner, but we had done a "do se do" several times in a circle dance. Okay, now I remember where we met before. I've seen you in Square Dance, but I don't think we've met. I'm Mark." She gave me her beautiful smile again, and said, "Hi Mark, I'm Lisa. Do you like square dancing? I love it. It gives me a little reprieve from all those other boring classes." "Yeah, I know what you mean, and yes, I agree.

It is a fun class." Nice to meet you Mark; I'll see you around." She left the library, but turned and waved, as she went out the door. I waved back and I thought, there's that smile again! After meeting Lisa in the library I watched for her in square dance class. I decided I would like to get to know her better, so made and effort to follow her out into the hallway at the end of class. "Hey Lisa," I called to her. "Wait up, I'll walk with you." She waited, and we walked across the campus together. Our conversation was pleasant, and by the time we each went our own way, I felt very comfortable being with her. We said, goodbye, but I vowed I would carry this friendship a little further. The following day, Lisa waited at the door for me. After that day, walking together was a routine thing. She didn't seem to be in a group of girls or choose to walk with anyone other than me. On Friday after class, I asked her to join me for a drink at the   drive-in. She readily accepted, but we agreed we would not be able to stay there long, as both of us needed to get home. I had chores to do, and her drive was twenty miles away. But at least I had made some progress in my pursuit of this new friendship. I had never dated a girl except Carla, and she kept flashing across my mind.

Why was I having a problem with dating Lisa? Carla had told me in no uncertain terms that she was not ready for steady dating. Why did I feel guilt over being attracted to another girl? No strings were attached to my deep friendship with Carla; I definitely had a problem. True, I had always thought that sometime in the future Carla and I would enter into a serious relationship that might even lead to marriage. This was only in my day-dreaming, because to this point we had never discussed the future, but in some strange way, we had let our friendship grow deeper and deeper to the point that we actually needed each other. I lectured myself about my guilt in wanting to date Lisa. After all I had only met Lisa briefly, and knew very little about her, except that I liked her personality and of course her smile. The solution to that problem would be to go on a date; get to know her better. We each drove our cars to the A&W and parked side by side. I motioned to her to sit in my car, which she did. We ordered Root

Beer Floats, brought them into the car and because of the cold January wind, rolled the window up, and started drinking our floats. I started the conversation by saying, "I guess I was hungrier that I thought. This drink really hits the spot. How about you?" "Right, I didn't eat much lunch, so was looking forward to getting something into my empty stomach." It only took those few words to break the ice, and we were on the way to an interesting, open question and answer session frequently with little jokes that kept us laughing.

Our drinks were finished much too soon and we had to end our date and start home. We agreed that it was fun and that we should visit the A&W again.

My father called with the news that Kati came through the surgery, but she was still under the effect of the anesthesia, and that as soon as he was sure about Kati's condition, he would be coming home. Mom and Kati of course would stay in Rochester about two weeks until Kati could travel. I was relieved that the surgery was over, and especially welcomed the news that Dad would be home soon. The time was drawing near for mid-term exams, and I desperately needed to spend more time on my studies. Algebra and English were the two required subjects I had to spend extra time on. I can't imagine why Algebra, as related to farming is an important subject, although I am sure in the future I will understand. My English professor assigns essays as half of the final grade, so it is important that I write an essay that will get me a passing grade. My problem is choosing the subject. When I have decided on what the essay subject will be, the writing will be easy. Actually, I need Carla to give me some advice about my school work. "Carla, Carla, why do you have to be so far away when I need to talk?" I asked, knowing full well, she was almost two hundred miles away. Here I am calling for Carla, when Lisa is the one I see and admire on a daily basis. "Get Carla off your mind, Mark, there are other girls in town." I lectured myself.

I had not seen the Nelsons, Carla's parents, since she was home at Christmas time, so I decided to stop in at the J.C. Penny store, where Mr. Nelson was manager. I was in need of a pair of jeans; I was looking through them for my size, when someone said, "Hello Mark." I turned and there was Carla's father giving me his welcome customer smile. I returned his greeting with, "Hi Mr. Nelson, what a nice surprise!" In fact, it was no surprise at all, because I planned the store trip, hoping he would be helping customers, rather than upstairs in his office. I thought, "What a liar you are Mark, but maybe God will forgive you this time." "May I help you find some jeans, Mark?" He found some jeans I liked, but I was thinking; "Never mind the jeans Mr. Nelson, let's talk about Carla."

We visited about the weather, school, I told him about Kati's surgery, and finally I asked if he had heard from Carla recently. He said, "We called her yesterday to let her know that we are leaving on our winter trip this week-end. She was fine, sounded like she is studying a lot . Those teachers in Montana are great on reading assignments, so she has more reading to do than she likes. I sure miss my daughter, Mark. She was such a little tom boy, she and I spent lots of time riding horses, and having fun. I felt like she was the boy I never had." "I'm sure you do miss her Mr. Nelson. I think Sapphire and Harmony miss her too! I need to be on my way, so hope you and Mrs Nelson have a wonderful vacation." I paid for my jeans and hurried home.

The wind was blowing, and the sky took on a cloudy overcast look. A storm was blowing in and I still needed to get my work in the barnyard finished before dark, which was approaching fast. I gave the animals extra feed and water in case the storm proved to be a big one, and I would not be able to tend them come morning. I did not plan on driving through snow-drifts and getting stalled as I had done only two weeks ago. I had learned my lesson; no more taking chances.

I turned the T.V. on, hoping to get news of the weather where my father was traveling. It seemed that the storm blowing in was not limited to our own area, but was wide spread. If Dad left early Saturday morning, he would be somewhere near the Denver area. Mountain driving during and after a storm was usually very treacherous. I sincerely hoped that my father would use better judgement than I had when I hit that snowdrift. I had a neighbor that rescued me, but my father was traveling a sparcely traveled mountain road, and the chance of getting help would be remote.

After eating dinner, I turned the T.V. to the weather station for more information about the weather. It was not good. A heavy snow had fallen over the mountains, and the temperature was minus thirty degrees. People were being warned not to travel over the mountain passes. Only large trucks or those who had two-way radios should be on the road. I turned the T.V. off and went to my room to study. The wind was howling; I heard different noises of things being blown around outside, and my mind was a jumble of thoughts. Were all the gates shut and fastened securely, so that none of the animals could get out, did I leave enough water in the troughs? I finally dropped off into a deep sleep. No more worrying about my responsibilities. I slept like a baby! I have no idea how babies sleep, but I grew up hearing Mother use that same phrase; "sleep like a baby."

So what, if I admit that I slept like a baby. I turned my car radio on and went to school. Things were looking up for me at last. Kati and Mother would be home in a few days. My father was on the road heading home, I had taken care of the ranch in a way that I thought would be pleasing to my parents, and I had met Lisa.

Father would be home Sunday, just two days from now. I checked my map, tracing the route he was traveling, and figured he was probably somewhere near the Badlands of South Dakota. That entire area was under bitter cold conditions. It would be a huge relief to see that truck of his pull into the driveway.

I looked across the room in square dance class and saw Lisa looking in my direction. I waved to her, motioning toward to door, signaling her that I wanted to talk after class. This was Friday and,what better time to ask for a date? The movie showing at our local drive-in was Dr. Zhivago, a new movie, with many credits. It might not be a perfect movie to take a date to, but my choices were limited. The only, indoor theater was showing a western, besides who wants to go to an indoor movie on a date.

I had not been lucky enough to get in a dance set, where Lisa and I would "swing or, do se do" together, so when class was over I made a dash for the door . Lisa was waiting for me. "Hey Lisa, wait up," I called to her. She gave one of her welcome smiles. "What are you doing tonight? How about a movie ? That is if you don't already have a date." I was holding my breath for her answer. Why no, Mark, as a matter of fact I don't." My ole heart gave a leap, and I said, "Great, that's great! I thought we could go to the drive-in. I heard on the radio that the drive-in was open on weekends." "Sounds like fun to me, Mark. As you know, that berg I live in doesn't have a theatre, indoor or outdoor, so I don't see many movies. Lisa's father operated a small cafe, in conjunction with the bus station, so I knew what she meant when she called Deaver a berg.

"Okay Lisa, I'll drive to Deaver and pick you up about seven." "No, no, Mark, you won't need to make that long drive. My grandmother lives in Powell. I usually stay with her when I have somewhere in Powell to go. I'm always welcome there and I love my grandmother very much. So just pick me up there. I'll write the address down." After digging in her purse, finding something to write on, she finally handed me the directions. I was relieved that I didn't have to make the long drive to Deaver to pick her up, and drive her home after the movie. "Thanks, Lisa, I'll see you tonight." We each went our way. I could not believe that I actually had a date with someone other than Carla.

Lisa was fun to be with, and both of us enjoyed the movie. The weather was a bit chilly, so I turned he car heater on, but did not want to run the battery down. When I turned the motor off, the car cooled off giving me a good excuse to put my arm around her, which was a signal to do a bit of cuddling to stay warm, but this being our first date, I was careful about getting too cozy. We enjoyed popcorn and cokes, laughed about school things, and generally enjoyed the evening. I was a perfect gentleman; walked her to the door, thanked her for a fun evening, and headed back to my car. When I was half-way down the walk, I turned and waved good-night. While driving home, my thoughts were a jumble. Lisa had a totally different personality than Carla. She was relaxed, funny, and much less serious. I enjoyed her company, but just how serious did I want this new relationship to be.

When Carla crossed my mind, I realized how much I was neglecting Sapphire and Harmony. Tomorrow I will ride, and ride I did; as soon as the animals were taken care of I saddled Sapphire and headed for the prairie. She was in excellent shape. I tried her at every speed I thought she needed practice in. We galloped, trotted, walked and loped. I was glad she was in good shape for training. The 4th of July race at the fair was only a few months off, and winning that race meant going to the state fair in Billings where a large sum of money went to the winners. I also took Harmony out; she was in good shape for not having been ridden since I rode her back to the corral after Kati's accident. I rode her bare- back, as she was still skittish about having a saddle on.

Thankfully, our hired man, Tony, was back from his vacation to Mexico, where he visited his family every year. Now I could depend on his help. We had fences to repair, hay to be hauled to the pasture; many large jobs, which I had saved for his return. Dad would be home soon and I could place the responsibility on him, where it belonged.

Sunday was a fairly restful day. I finished chores, took Sapphire and Harmony for a few laps around the corral, and even made them feel good with a grooming brush. As late evening came, I began to look for my dad to drive in, but no sign of him. When seven o'clock came and he was not here, I began to worry. The later it became the more desperate I became. I decided to place a call to my mother. She assured me that he had left at the planned time and reminded me how my dad felt about long distance calls. "You know, son, how your father is about calling long distance. Regardless of his phone phobia, I feel sure if something was wrong, he would call you." "I guess you are right, Mom, he will probably show up here in a few minites." I hung the phone up, feeling somewhat relieved. I had plenty of homework that needed to be done, so I went to my room and dug into that big stack of books.

Monday morning as I was driving from the barnyard toward the house, a car turned into the lane that led to the the house. Who is coming to see me this early in the morning? I thought, all the neighbors and friends know my parents are in Minnesota, so what is going on? I pulled in to the parking space beside the parked car. It was then that I noticed the sign on the side that told me it was the sheriff. He had knocked on the front door, and getting no response turned and was walking toward my car . "Hey Sheriff, what brings you out in these parts so early in the day?" He greeted me back, and came forward to meet me. "Well, Mark, maybe we should go inside to get out of this cold wind." I agreed and apologized for my house-keeping; all the time getting more curious as to why the sheriff was here! " Mark," he said, "I think you need to sit down for this." I motioned to a couple of chairs, and we sat down. "Mark," he seemed to be stalling about something, " There has been an accident, it's your Dad, Mark, he had an accident." By now, my heart was pounding, and I could barely speak. "But he's okay, right? Where is he? I could see the sorrow in the sheriff's face, and knew right away that my father was not alright. "No Mark, he's, he's dead." "You 've got to be kidding sheriff, I don't believe you." My heart was pounding like it would explode, my head was whirling, and I felt faint. My eyes were blurry, the sheriff seemed far away. Finally the sheriff said, "No Mark, we think your father suffered a heart attack, while driving. We aren't sure yet what happened, but a patrolman came upon his car, motor still running, off to the side of the road, as if he tried to stop, but ended up a few feet off to the side, headed toward a steep embankment. We are not sure about the heart attack, but we will know more about that as soon as a doctor examines him." By now I had gained my composure and simply said, "Slow down, Sheriff, I don't need to hear anymore detail now. My father is dead and that is all I can take right now. I put my head down between my arms let my shock and grief go through my body and sobbed uncontrollably. When I raised my head, the sheriff was standing, his hat in hand, preparing to leave. "Mark I do need to ask you; shall we bring his body back to the funeral home in Powell?" I nodded my head, and uttered, "Yes, please do. There is something else sheriff, please do not let my mother hear of this until I can be with her. I will be leaving in a couple of hours to Minnesota, and I need to be the one to give her this terrible news. We will travel back together and then face our duties after we get home." "Okay Mark, I will try my best to honor your wish, and good luck getting to Billings and a plane out to Rochester. If I can be of any help, please feel free to ask. See you later," and he was gone.

I thought, "am I being irrational or impulsive by going to Mother and Kati? I have never been as upset as I am now, but irrational? I really don't think so. I think my judgment in this decision is sound. I think my mother and Kati need to hear this heartbreaking news from me. They will need me. I'm going as soon as I can get ready." I started making plans for the care of the animals immediately. I drove to Tony's house, knocked on the door. When he answered the door, he looked at me and in his broken English said, "What is wrong, Mark?" I'm sure I was still trembling and had very little color in my face. "Tony," I blurted out. "I know you are still on vacation, but I need your help. Dad had a heart attack. It was bad, Tony, He didn't make it; he is dead." I could see the shock, and disbelief on his face. Tears came to his eyes, and when I saw his tears, I felt the tears returning to my eyes. After all, this man had worked for our family for many years. He was almost like family. When he regained his composure, he said, "Mark, what can I do? What do you need?" I explained my plans for going to Rochester, to be with Mom and Kati, that I was driving to Billings to catch a plane, and that he would be responsible for caring for the animals, and that I would call Abe and ask him to help or give advice if he needed it. Tony expressed his deep sorrow. "Mark, you know I will do my best to take care of things around here. How long will you be gone?" "Tony, I am not sure. Three or four days at the most. Just don't hesitate to call on Abe for help if you need it." He assured me again he would do his best. I left feeling a sense of relief that we had such a dependable worker and friend in Tony. Although Tony's work was usually in the field, he had been around the barnyard enough through the years to know what had to be done.

I rushed into the house and called Abe. I was thankful he answered the phone, otherwise I would have to leave a note on his door, which meant more time spent before getting on my way to Billings. Of course, I had to explain what had happened; that my father had suffered a heart attack and died, while on his way home from Minnesota. Abe and Mae had been our neighbors and friends since the very beginning of the homesteading days. Naturally, he was terribly shocked and saddened by the news, but seemed to understand my reasoning about being with Mother at this terrible time, "Mark, I will do anything to help you out, and will check in on Tony often. You take care, and I'll be in touch as soon as you get back." Again I felt some relief, knowing I could depend on our good neighbor.

I put a few things in a small bag, gassed my car from the large tank we always kept for farm use, and was on my way to getting a flight out to Rochester without too much delay. I realized my chances were slim since I didn't have a reservation, but hoping upon hope that I would be lucky. After parking the car, I walked the long distance from long term parking to the airport . I had heard that some larger airports furnished a tram from the parking to the airport, but Billings was a small airport compared to NY or LA, so no luxuries. The teller at the ticket window said the seats were all taken, and my best chance was standby. I had no choice regardless of my situation. I bought a ticket and prepared to wait, perhaps as long as three hours or more. I sat on a bench next to an older man, who immediatly engaged me in a conversation. I was hesitant to talk, but finally returned his friendliness. I told him about my plight; going into detail about my fathers sudden death and the fact that I was trying to get to Minnesota to be with my mother. I could tell by the expression on his face, and the seriousness of his voice that he was a very compassionate person. When I finished my story; to my surprise he offered me his seat on the plane, explaining that he was on vacation and that a few hours delay would mean nothing to him. I argued with him about his inconvenience, but he insisted that he really wanted to do it. I accepted this kind stranger's offer, and in thirty minutes, I was on my way to meet Mother and Kati. I arrived at the Rochester Airport, took a taxi, and gave them the name of the motel where my family were staying; not having any kind of clue or idea of how I would break the terrible news of my father's death to them. I found their room and knocked on the door. I could see the shock on Mother's face when she saw me standing there. "Son!" she yelled, " What on earth are you doing here?" This was something that could not wait, so I plunged right into it. "Mom, I just decided to come. Lets sit down over here, so we can talk. How is Kati? Oh, Kati seems to be doing fine. She is in the other room asleep. She was only half smiling, and I am sure I could not maintain a happy look on my face. Mark, I'm sure you wanted to see Kati and I, but now be honest. Why are you here? I could not hold back the tears when I started to speak. I rose from my chair, stood closer to her chair, and blurted out; Mom, there has been an accident. Now the tears were rolling down my cheeks. An accident?" she asked, "What kind of accident Mark? Tell me, what happened. "Mom, it's Dad. He had a heart attack." "But he's alright, isn't he? Where is he Mark? "But Mom, no, he isn't alright. Mom he died." She looked at me for several seconds in disbelief, then screamed, no, no, it's not true, I don't believe it! Not my Bill, no, no, not my love; and then she broke down into uncontrollable sobbing. Her sobbing was heart wrenching, her entire body was shaking. I wrapped my arms around her and held her close. During the trip to Rochester, I had not let myself think about father, or that he was dead, but now all the grief I felt was coming out. As I held my mother close, we cried together. Finally I went to the bathroom and brought a small wet towel and wiped my mother's face. I helped her up and led her to the bed; all the time comforting her in every little way I could. I put two pillows under her head, rubbed her hands and arms, until the sobbing became quieter and she stopped shaking. When Kati came into the room from her rest, she saw me, and screamed, "Mark! What are you doing here? When she saw Mom on the bed, she ran to her, crying, "Mom, what's wrong? "Wait Kati, there has been an accident. I took her in my arms and broke the news about Father in much the same way as I had to Mother. She reacted as Mother had, but soon settled down and the three of us sat on the bed crying, holding each other, trying to come to grips with the unbelievable pain and grief that had suddenly come into our lives.

We sat round the small table in the motel room, each of us caught up in our own thoughts. Occasionally one of us would burst into tears, which soon subsided. After a time, which seemed like years; Mother spoke. " We need to get home, so we should try to get you a reservation. Kati and I have ours for tomorrow, but you need one. Mark, you are the strong one in the family now. I have a number to call, so try to call the Airport, and find out if they can get you on the same flight as Kati and I have. Maybe our luck will be with us in this. Most travelers will not be going north this time of year. Let's give it a try"

Mother went to her purse, and came back with tickets and the information that I needed to call. A cheerful voice answered and asked if she could help me. "Dear God, I prayed, I need help!" I'm sorry sir, there are no seats left on that flight. Is there anything else I can help you with?" I was desperate to get back home as soon as possible. I said, " Please miss, just hear me out. My father had a sudden heart attack and died. I desperately need to get to Billings, Montana. My sister recently had brain surgery at Mayo Clinic. We need to get home, to face our responsibilities there. Isn't there any way you can help me out here?" After being polite and listening to my story, the agent said. "This sounds like an emergency, so I will put you on stand-by. Quite often someone fails to show up and we can sell their seat, but you need to get to the airport plenty early in case you can get on." I thanked her politely, and hung up.

When we arrived at the airport the following morning early, I checked with the agent, explaining that I had been put on stand-by for flight # 294 to Billings. This time the agent was a man. He seemed surprised that we had come two hours early, and wasted no time in telling me the good news. "We actually do have a cancellation, son, let's get that ticket ready. You are very lucky!" When I returned to Mother and Kati, we all drew a breath of relief. Now we would be able to travel together. I was proud of both Mother and Kati with the way they were holding up during this very bad day, but knew what followed was going to be much harder. As for me, I felt a big load on my shoulders, and was trying hard to face up to it.

The flight to Billings, and the drive home were uneventful. I coaxed Mom and Kati into getting something to eat and they agreed. We had driven about ten miles when I spotted a small cafe called, "Ma's Home Cookin." We were surprised at how hungary we actually were. We enjoyed the home cooking offered, but ate in complete silence. Each of us with our own thoughts and memories of Dad.

Upon arriving home, after getting Mother and Kati settled, I went directly to the barnyard to check on the animals. Everything seemed to be in good shape. Water in the troughs, Sapphire and Harmony also had water, which surprised me, as their water had to be carried in buckets from the faucet to their shed. When I started to leave, our hired man, Tony drove in . I congratulated him on the good job he had done. He said Mr. Abe had come down once every day to check on things. I went back to the house to find Mother and Kati resting. Mother heard me come into the kitchen and came in. "Mark, I suppose we should get busy on some arrangements." "I know, Mom, but how?" "I would like you to call the funeral director and make an appointment for tomorrow morning. I'm sure he can help us get started. Mark, you are the strong one now, and I hate to put so much on your shoulders, but Kati certainly is not strong enough or able, and she is so young." She broke down again and began sobbing. "Don't worry Mom, I can do it!" I placed the call to Easton's Funeral Home and Mr. Easton himself answered. When I told him my name, he said, "Oh yes, Mark, I am so sorry about your Father. When can you come in?" We set a time for the next morning. When I placed the receiver down, I suddenly realized how very tired I was. I needed some supper and a night's rest. I suggested to my Mother that we eat food out of the freezer, as I had stored up plenty of good things while she was away. When supper was over, we all fell into bed. We had a big heartbreaking day ahead of us tomorrow.

Mother and I kept our appointment with Mr. Easton. He was a very gracious man who treated us as close friends or family. He remembered my father from their visits at the Elks Club, where they were both members. We took care of all arrangements, with Mr. Easton guiding us along, which made our decisions much easier. After the mortuary, we made a stop at the church to ask our minister, Rev. Carter to handle the services. By the time we finshed taking care of the funeral arrangements, I could see that Mother was exhausted. I drove straight home and insisted that she get some much needed rest. Kati was still rcovering from the long trip home. She tired easily; in fact she was still recuperating from the surgery, and the shock of father's sudden death. We cautioned her about getting overly tired, and that resting was more important than she probably realized. She would be traveling to the clinic for a follow up check on the surgery results in two weeks, so it was important that she get a lot of rest. Hopefully she would be released from the specialist to her doctor in Billings for future care. The funeral was over, and Dad's car was to be brought home from Rapid City, South Dakota, where it had been in storage since my fathers death. Now it was time for me to get back into school. I would have to work extra hard to catch up with my assignments. I had missed one week of school, and I had doubts that I could get all the over-due assignments in and pass my finals.

The grief of losing my father was over-whelming. Mother broke into tears at the very mention of his name, and Kati simply refused to face the truth about our dad; that he was gone, and would not be coming home any minute. For these reasons; concentrating on books was difficult. I would explain to my professors the reason for not being in class, although I am certain they had heard or read in the paper about Father's death. Hopefully they would be understanding and allow me some leeway.

Carla came home for a short time to attend the funeral. When I saw her there, I thought I was seeing a ghost, that my imagination was working overtime, but when she worked her way through the crowd and greeted me with a big hug, I knew it was no ghost. " I'm so sorry, Mark. I had to come. When my mother called and told me the news, I didn't hesitate one minute; I could not let you go through this without seeing you. So here I am. I have to leave tomorrow, but maybe we can meet somewhere for a visit before I go." She was holding both my hands in hers, and I wanted so badly to take her in my arms, but of course, this was not the time or place. "Okay Carla, come to the corral in the morning. I will be doing chores. We can have a visit, then go to my house for breakfast. I feel sure my Mom would love to see you. Also, you will get to see Sapphire and Harmony." She agreed the plan sounded like a good one. She looked across the room and her mother waved to her. They were ready to leave. We said good-bye, and she joined her parents.

When Carla left with her parents, I realized how much I had missed her. Even though her personality was totally different to Lisa's, and I enjoyed doing fun things with Lisa, but holding her in my arms and kissing her good night, which was a normal part of dating, only made me feel guilt about dating anyone but Carla. When Carla arrived at the corral, I was busy carrying water to the horses. I motioned her to come to the shed where Sapphire and Harmony were housed. She commented on what a nice job I was doing, caring for our horses. They were free to run around the corral as much as they chose, or they could just stand soak up the warm sunshine. She was eager to have school out for the summer, so we could really work on their running time, and have Sapphire ready for the big Fair Race. She joined Mother and I for a breakfast. of scrambled eggs and ham, with some of Mom's delicious bisquits. We were thanking Mom for the wonderful breakfast and getting ready to go back to the corral, when Kati came into the room. She was surprised to see Carla, and especially that she had joined us for breakfast. Kati rubbed her sleepy eyes and actually acted a little perturbed that she had not been awakened in time to join us for breakfast. Mother explained, "Kati sweetheart, you know I was only following doctors orders for you to get plenty of rest. I promise, if Carla comes again we will wake you." Carla walked to the door where Kati stood and gave her a big hug. "Kati, I'm so happy to see you, you look great. We will take some nice long rides this summer while I am home." She gave Kati another hug, kissed her good-bye, and we headed for the corral.

Chapter 10
THE DECISION

SAPPHIRE AND Harmony had not been ridden for several days, and Harmony did not like the idea of a saddle so I rode her bareback and Carla rode Sapphire. The ride was leisurely, no racing or challenges. This was Carla I was with, and I was finally able to give in to my feelings about father's death and what the future might hold for me. Mother and I had not discussed how we would deal with the ranch without my dad, but I knew the time was drawing near for us to make plans. My grief was deep; almost unbearable. I could not hold the tears back. All the time I was thinking of my Mom, and how she would endure the years ahead. Not realizing that I had drifted into serious thought. Carla brought me out of my trance, when she said, "Mark, I know how you are hurting, and I simply do not have enough words in my heart to tell you how much I care. I wish I lived closer to offer the comfort you need."

When I looked into her face, I could see tears of compassion and love. At that moment I knew that someday this girl would be my wife, but I also knew how serious she felt about her education, and that I would be waiting a long time before I could hold her in my arms and tell her my feelings.

We had been riding and talking two hours, and I hated for the ride to end, I said, "Carla, you must know how much it means to me to "pour my heart" out to an understanding friend like you, but it's time now to turn these horses around and get back; you to your family and friends in town, and me to my mother and sister.

I walked in the door, and the sight I saw was not an encouraging one, Kati on the couch sleeping, and Mom was sitting in her favorite lounge chair, with her head back, and eyes closed. I said, "Hey Mom, what are you doing?" She waved to me to come closer, and put her hand out for me to hold. Instead I kneeled beside her and put my arms around her shoulders. She leaned into me, and whispered, "Son, I don't think I can make it without your Dad. I'm sorry I can't be more cheerful, but I think you understand." Yes, Mother, I do understand, probably more than you think I do, but we have to be brave, and take care of the ranch like Dad would want us to. This ranch was his life, his dreams, his happiness, and of course you, Kati and me." As I talked, Mother's spirits seemed to return a bit. Yes son, but I don't know whether we can continue running the farm without your Dad, and I do want you to get your education." "I know, I know, and I have given those things a lot of thought. The thing is, I have chosen ranching as my future. Agriculture is my major in college. If we choose to quit ranching, what will I do with my life? Everything is here for me. I think the best thing we can do is to give it our best and if we fail, that will be the time to throw in the towel. Of course the decision is all yours, but this is the way I feel." Mom sat in her recliner, with her eyes closed for several minutes. Finally she looked at me with tears in her eyes and said, "Mark, you are a loving son, a brave boy, hard working; I trust you with all my heart, so let's do it. We will give it a try. When the time comes for you to go away to a larger college, if we have failed, we will make other plans. I gave my mother a big hug and said," I'm sure we won't fail, Mom, you made the right decision." Jokingly I added, "How could two "big brains" like ours go wrong? Now, how about one of your special dinners to celebrate our decision?" I took her hands, pulled her up and led her into the kitchen. She gave me one of her wonderful smiles, that I had not seen since long before my dad's death, and hoped with all my heart to see more often.

Tomorrow a new semester begins, meaning I soon would have one year of college finished. I missed riding and training Sapphire and Harmony, so now, I must get serious, especially with Sapphire. I had promised Billy the last time we exchanged words, that Sapphire would win the big Fourth of July race. Her training was up to me; with some help from Kati, until Carla was out of school in May. The days were beginning to get longer which meant more daylight hours, so I would be able work with Sapphire after school, and Harmony on week-ends.

When I was in high school I could not have been less serious about learning or making decent grades, but college is different. My future depends on making good grades, so I can pass the entry exam to the University of WY for a degree in Agriculture. Now that I have the responsibility of a ranch to manage, I need to be able to practice new farming technology to succeed on a modern ranch.

After my sister, Kati's accident, we felt that riding a school bus would be tiring for her, so she rode to school with me. My classes ended an hour before hers, so I had time for library work or better yet, occasionally, I could spend and hour talking with Lisa, or drinking a root-beer at the A&W.

The time was nearing for Kati to return to Mayo Clinic for a visit to her specialist, Dr. Wilcox. The trip would be expensive, also we had many plans to make about transportation. It would be much easier if we could ask Dr. Wilcox to simply talk to the Doctor in Billings, or send a copy of his report. Kati was showing signs of complete recovery by gaining strength, no more headaches and an excellent appetite. I often joked with her about how much food she could eat and not gain weight. "Hey Sis, save some for me!" When I kidded her, she would point her fork like she was going to throw it at me. "Mark," she said, "Go jump in the lake and swallow a snake!" Back to normal, eh kid." Then seriously, "how about holding the time-watch, while I ride Sapphire around the arena?" "Oh Mark, you are such a crazy brother. You got it! I'll be there." My father and I built the riding arena when I was training Nochi for races. Now, it will be used again.

Chapter 11
LISA

WHEN MOM raised the subject of Kati's trip to Rochester, she began by saying the same thing I had been thinking. "How can we do this trip, Mark? I am considering making a call to Dr. Dominic in Billings and see if he agrees that a report by phone and of course a printed copy would be satisfactory, rather than a trip to Rochester, MN. I was relieved that we were both thinking along the same lines. I quickly agreed, "I have been thinking about that trip and am glad you have the same idea. Yes, go ahead and give it a try. I am sure Dr. Dominic will make a sensible decision." "Okay Mark, I'll call this afternoon. I'm sure Kati would love to get on a plane and fly again, but she is too young to think about the many problems we have facing us if we travel by plane. She has her whole life to fly, and we simply cannot afford to fly. Hopefully, we can get those results with much less time and expense. I will make that call soon, so we know what to plan on."

As soon as I entered the Gym, where we held Square Dance classes, I looked across the room and spotted Lisa. She waved to me to come to her set. The class was evenly divided between boys and girls, so each girl or boy would have a partner of the opposite sex. The set she had been placed in was one boy short, so Lisa waited for me to be her partner. Of course I accepted with a great deal of enthusiasm. Lisa was not a tall girl, probably five feet six inches, where I stood well above her head with my six foot height. Lisa's interest outside of college was dancing. She started ballet when she was five years old, and it became a very large part of her life. Her mother had a dance studio, so Lisa was involved in a small way with the studio. On the other hand, my life revolved around horses. We talked dance and then switched to horses. I knew absolutely nothing about ballet and she knew very little about horses. Our friendship grew in a completely different way than the friendship I had with Carla.

Carla would be home for the summer and we could spend hours together; but I was in a real dilemma. Certainly my love life did not take priority over my duties at the ranch, but It was in my thoughts more than I liked to admit. Lisa and Carla; Carla and Lisa. Sometime I would have to make an important decision.

We sat down for dinner and Mother couldn't wait to break the good news. "Good news kids, I had a call from Doctor Dominic this afternoon and guess what he said Kati? The report of your surgery from Dr. Wilcox to Dr Dominic was great. The surgery was successful. No sign of bleeding, so you have been released to the care of Dr. Dominic in Billings. You will have to have another check-up in six months, but you are free to ride, and go to parties; with my consent of course. You can be a normal girl now." Kati was elated as was I. Mother continued, "And I have prepared a special desert to celebrate the good news. How does strawberry short cake sound? I found some frozen strawberries buried beneath a bunch of other things in the freezer today and I know how much you kids love my special strawberry desert, so these hands got busy and here it is. Enjoy!" Without thinking I started to say, "Remember it was also Dad's favorite." but caught myself, knowing it would bring tears to Mother's eyes. Hopefully, someday we can speak about my dad, but that time has not come yet. Mother and Dad were very close, and I know it will be months or years before she will be back to the cheerful Mother my sister, Kate and I knew before my dad's death.

I enjoyed Lisa's company; her cheerful smile, and the laughs we had when we were together. "How about a movie tomorrow night, Lisa?" I asked as we left square dance class. "Thanks, Mark, and the answer is yes, I will be thrilled to go. When I arrived I went to the door, hoping Lisa would not expect me to come in, but instead she invited me in to meet her grandmother. She was very polite. and had the same smile that had attracted me to Lisa the first time I saw her. We exchanged a bit of pleasant conversation, then she said in a jovial way, "Now you kids get out of here Lisa, I don't think your friend came to spend the evening with me. "so go to your movie and enjoy!! "The movie we watched was "Picnic" staring Cliff Robertson. The evening went pretty much the same as our last date . We drank cokes, munched on popcorn and chatted whenever there was a lull in the movie. I had my arm around her during much of the time. She responded by moving closer to me and often leaned her head on my shoulder. I enjoyed the cuddling, but made no advances, such as kissing. When we arrived at her grandmother's house, I walked her to the door, and before I knew what was happening, she put her arms around my neck, and then it happened. We were kissing passionately again and again. All thoughts of Carla went out the window and I was having the time of my life. I continued to date Lisa every Saturday night, and our relationship grew into something more passionate than I could have possibly imagined having with Carla. Yet a feeling of guilt came over me after each date. Carla and I had shared our problems for over three years. We had known some very happy times. We had developed a respect and companionship, that I could not dream of having with Lisa. I was expecting Carla home for the summer soon and I knew we would be spending hours daily riding and training Sapphire for the big race. How could I have fallen into a situation such as this? If my father was still alive, we would have a man-to-man talk, as we had done more times than I can remember. I talked to him candidly, and he was helpful, but certainly not critical. He simply guided me in the right direction. Suddenly a deep feeling of grief engulfed me; "Mark, stop this Dad is dead and you no longer have him to talk to I thought." I tuned the radio to some lively music and pressed on the gas peddle and hurried home.

I had plenty of problems without taking time to worry about girls. Calving time was here. We already had ten calves born without any complications, but occasionally, a mother needed help with the birth. Of course Doc Lee was always ready and willing to come when I called. We never got through a calving season without having him out at least three times. Our hired man Tony, proved to be indispensable. He had taken on a more responsible attitude after father's death, and actually proved to know a great deal more about the ranch than when Dad was alive to give him instructions on each job he was assigned to do.

I'm sure he realized the pressure my mother and I felt in being left to manage a three hundred acre ranch without my dad. A couple of our neighbors were so positive that we would fail, they offered to buy the ranch. Mother in a very tactful way let them know that the only way she would sell the place would be if we actually became homeless. I'm sure the word will get around in the neighborhood that we are in for the long haul, regardless of our inexperience. Nothing will stop us. We are staying here because it is our home, and that is what my father would expect us to do.

Amazing as it seems, our crops are beautiful. When I look across the fields and see acres and acres of green, swaying in the breeze, then glance up at the huge red ball, slowly dropping behind the mountains that have hovered over the valley since the rising of the sun. I feel the emotion my parents felt when as a young couple they made the decision to make northern Wyoming their home.

School will be out in a week, and Carla will be home for the summer. The relief of being out of school, coupled with Carla taking over much of the training of Sapphire for the race, certainly will give me more time for work and management of the ranch. Tony enlisted two members of his extended family from Mexico to assist with irrigation, and other field work. We housed them in a small house trailer. Since I do not speak Spanish, I gave instructions to Tony and he relayed them to our workers. I appreciated Tony and the progress he had made in taking responsibility for the workings of the ranch. Mother was also fond of Maria, Tony's wife and often called on her to help with household chores. With my father's encouragement, both Tony and Maria had gained U.S. citizenship. The decision to apply for citizenship came a few years ago, when Maria's mother became very ill. Maria rushed to Mexico to help care for her mother, but when she was ready to return to the states she found that she was not allowed to cross the border. Tony would either go back to Mexico to live with his wife, or find illegal passage for her to cross the border. Tony borrowed money from my parents and eventually Maria was transported across the border. It was at this time that my father encouraged, in fact insisted, that they apply for citizenship. After some months of studying, they passed the exam; at last they were citizens.

The school term ended, and Carla will be home in a week. In spite of all the set-backs I had during the semester, I passed all my classes; some with only a C grade, but Mother and I were satisfied with my C's and B's and thankful I had finished my first year of college. I could plan on going another year, but as far as attending the university to obtain a full four year degree, I really have doubts. I cannot imagine being away from the ranch full time. The ranch needs me and I definitely need it. When summer's end comes, Mother and I will mull the situation over and make a decision. My mom was still deep in grief over losing her life-long companion. She prepared nice meals for Kati and me, but ate very little herself. She was slowly losing weight, and many nights when she was in her room and the house was quiet, I heard her sobbing . One of these evenings, I grabbed a robe, went to her room and tapped lightly on her bedroom door. In a weak voice, she called to me to come in. I sat on the side of her bed, took her hand in mine, and said, "Mom, I am so sorry." If there is anything Kati or I can do to help you through this, please tell me." "No son, you and Tony have harvested some good crops, all this years calves are growing and healthy; I am so very proud of you." She reached for a tissue to wipe her tears and between more tears and sighs, said, " I just don't think I can make it without your Dad. Everything around reminds me of him. I awake in the night and feel for his body near mine. At this time in my life, I don't think I will ever be happy again." "Okay Mom, I have some ideas. I know it will not be easy, but we need to clear Dad's clothes out of the closet. Kati and I will help. We will give them to the Salvation Army. We will redecorate your bedroom, buy new carpet, paint, put up new curtains. Even buy a new bed, so when you move back in it will be a completely new room. While we are getting all that done, you should visit your sister in Maryland. I am sure Aunt Beth would love to have you visit, maybe two weeks, giving us time to get your bedroom finished. How does that plan sound?" "Mark, it sounds like a dream, but I will need o give it a little thought. I will see what Kati thinks. She still misses her Dad, as much as you and I do, so it matters to me what her reaction will be about me being away so long. Who knows? She may enjoy the idea of doing some cooking and house cleaning." "Great Mom, think it over and if you decide to go, we'll take it from there, Then we can start making plans for your trip and the redecorating project." She spoke softly; tears gone and said, "Thank you son, I think I can sleep now."

I awakened this Saturday morning to see the sun shining through my window. What a beautiful day welcomed me. The sun was slowly rising like a big round red ball over Heart Mountain; turning the chill in the air to a warm comfortable feeling that was rare here in northern Wyoming, where we are often greeted daily by a strong breeze, or occasionally by a forceful demanding; "blow your hat off " wind. But this is early June, when for a very short time winter disappears and summer shows it's face. It was a time for looking to the distance at green fields of growing crops and cattle grazing peacefully in pastures of lush green grass.

Tony was in charge of watering the crops, and harvest time not yet here. I felt free after my barnyard chores were finished to put a saddle on Sapphire, or Harmony and ride for hours. I followed the same trail I rode as a boy, several miles down a well trodden path where stood a large oak tree, with a creek nearby. The same place where Nochi was found after she escaped from the corral during a fierce thunder and lightening storm. The place where I stayed by her side until she could be led home. The place where we buried her under the large oak tree. I had wonderful memories of my childhood and Nochi. Now I am an adult, but I often remember, as a twelve year old boy, my very first night alone except for my injured horse as a companion, and how faithfully I tended my Nochi.

After the doctor released Kati and gave her the freedom to live a normal life, she immediately wanted to ride Harmony, but with the understanding that she never go riding alone. She readily agreed that her past experience was not something that she would care to repeat. She could only go if Carla or I was with her. Carla would arrive home today; Sunday, but would be busy until about Wednesday. It would be great to have her back; in charge of getting Sapphire ready for the big race. After all, Sapphire was Carla's horse, but Harmony belonged to me because Nochi was Harmony's sire. Since Nochi's death I did not have a horse, so instead of paying me money for Nochi fathering Sapphire's colt, I chose to take the colt. I suggested we call Sapphire's baby, Harmony. Harmony was Kati's favorite horse. She had been with me, and actually helped me when we placed the reins on, and again when Harmony wore her first saddle. Kati loved Harmony, and had watched her grow from a tiny colt into the beautiful mare she had become. But after the unfortunate accident which sent Kati to the hospital, she had not ridden. She was well now and could ride again. I can hear her begging, "Mark, come on, are we going to ride today? Is Carla coming out?" "Never satisfied," I thought! "this kid sister of mine. Will she always bug me, and then I remember how bad I felt when she lay in a coma in the hospital. After all she is still a kid." "Yeah Kati, you will get to ride. Carla will be home soon, and if I can't go, she will be more than happy to ride with you. Now don't bother me for a couple of days. Okay?" She responded by sticking her tongue out at me, but thought better of it, and said, "okay, okay, Mark, have it your way!"

Aunt Beth was overjoyed to have Mother come for a visit, and filled her with ideas of special things they would do during her two week visit. Mother called the Billings Airport and made the necessary round trip reservations to Bethesda, Maryland. She was to leave on Saturday the fourteenth of June and return June

28th. During her absence, Kati and I would be busy redecorating her bedroom. We were excited about our project; something neither of us had ever taken part in, so we had a lot to learn about painting, shopping for carpet and buying a new bed. Saturday rolled around much faster than I expected, and it was time for Kati and me to drive Mom to Billings to board the plane for Maryland. She and Kati had tears in their eyes when she left, but I had spent so much time alone while Kati was in the hospital that I no longer dreaded having her gone, and hopefully Kati would try her hand at cooking some of our meals. I was hoping that we would not have to live on frozen food although Mom had cooked a good supply.

Chapter 12
DOUBLE TROUBLE

T HE PHONE rang, and as usual Kati made a dash for it. "Mark it's for you." I was surprised to hear Lisa's voice. "How's it going out your way, Mark? I think about you all the time." I had to admit to Lisa that I had been very busy and explained about Mother leaving and the redecorating project I was undertaking, hoping she would not expect a date for at least two weeks. She was silent a while, then said, "I am sure you have good excuses, but it only takes a minute to place a call Mark, and I miss you so much! When will I see you again?" I admired Lisa for her uninhibited personality, but this time I felt pushed into a corner. With Carla back home, Lisa calling, my promise to Mom; I was overwhelmed; how could I have let myself get into such a quandary without hurting some of the people who meant so much to me? Surely there was a way. I just had to fnd it. "Okay Lisa," I spoke after I had mentally gone over my predicament. "I miss our dates too, and I think you know why, but those kisses will just have to wait a few days. I will call you in about ten days and we can plan a date." "Okay Mark, she answered, but I don't like it. Until then I guess I will have to be satisfied with memories." She hung up before I could say a loving good -bye.

Carla arrived home Sunday. Her parents drove to Missoula to help bring the many things home that college girls seem to think they need. I expect her to visit Sapphire, Harmony and me this week. In less than a month we must have Sapphire ready to race at the big county fair on July 4th. I'm sure Billy will have his horse, Trigger, in the race, and since Sapphire is his strongest competition, no doubt he is spending many hours daily at the fairground training his horse. Carla and I are every bit as intent on winning as Billy is, so it will be an exciting race. The winner, not only has the honor of being the best, but will receive a $1000.00 prize, and the honor of going on to the state fair in Billings, Montana

Kati and I drove to Cody today to shop for the things we needed to decorate Mom's room. We choose a very light blue paint for the walls, with a darker shade of carpet, which would be delivered and laid when we finished the painting. After the walls and carpet were done, we would choose curtains and the bed. I was pleasantly surprised to find how many excellent ideas my sister contributed to our "project" as we referred to it. I have to admit that my kid sister matured a lot during her illness; I can't believe she will be a Junior in high school this fall.

Kati and I went for a ride today. After we returned I ask Kati to check Sapphire's time around the corral. Three laps around the riding arena is equal to one mile. Sapphire made three laps in three minutes, which tells me she has a long way to go before she will be ready for the race. Kati was filling the water trough with the hose that reached from the faucet to the animal drinking trough, and I was carrying buckets of water to the horse shed, when to my surprise Carla drove in and honked the horn of her little yellow Volkswagon. I dropped the buckets and ran to meet her. I grabbed her in my arms and kissed her lightly on the cheek. She was happy to stay wrapped in my arms, but soon spotted Kati coming toward us. She gave Kati a big smile and a hug, then we headed for the corral to visit Sapphire, and Harmony. When Carla looked at me with those beautiful brown eyes I saw in them the love she carried in her heart for me. I saw the unselfishness and faithfulness I had experienced from her time and again through the years of our friendship. I thought, "How can I not love this girl? Her unwavering devotion to the goals we had for the future meant everything to me, but I had made love to someone else I cared for in a completely different way. Lisa was fun loving, affectionate, and the physical urge I had for her when we were together was beyond control. I was sure she shared my feelings. I would be with her again tomorrow night, and I wanted that date!"

When Carla was ready to leave I held her in my arms far longer than I ever had before. I reached for her face, brought her lips to mine and we kissed passionately. Yes, my Carla had, as she said earlier, "Mark, you will see, I have changed." We walked hand in hand to her car. She was gone for now, but I knew I wanted her back.

Kati and I drove to Billings to meet Mom at the airport. Her trip was a success, but she was thrilled to be home . She seemed happier than before she left; thanks to the efforts of Aunt Beth to keep her busy with sight seeing and visiting. The trip was a perfect medicine for my grieving Mother. When she stepped into her bedroom and saw all the changes she shed tears of happiness. "I love it, really love it. I can't imagine how all this redecorating was done in such a short time." I could have said, "Well I do Mom, we worked our tails off to get it done." But instead both Kati and I were overjoyed that our Mother was back to normal again after the tragedy of losing her love of many years, as well as her confidant and best friend. Of course, the sadness of losing our father would stay with us forever, but for our Mom, it was akin to losing her life.

My date with Lisa last night was wonderful. We had not seen each other for over two weeks. When she came to the door at her grandmothers home, she fell into my arms, and when I stepped back slightly, she whispered, "My grandmother's gone to a church meeting. She won't be home for hours." She led me to her bed, and we made love as never before. No movie, no A&W, just the two of us satisfying the longing we had built up for each other during the past two weeks apart. When I left, I promised to meet her again next Saturday night. One last kiss and I left.

The County Fair was only two weeks away, so Carla came every day spending hours working with Sapphire; riding her around the arena, and timing her each time. She was gaining in her speed with each time around. Sapphire was a thourough-bred quarter horse, so being bred from the same line of thourough-bred horses as Nochi, she had racing in her blood. Everyone who new her was sure with the right training she could win the big race. Of course Billy also had a great horse from racing stock, and he was an excellent trainer, so this race would be very close. Kati helped Carla with Sapphire, as I had duties with the crops, which were getting close to harvest time. Tony and his pals were doing a great job, but I still needed to oversee the watering, making sure some fields were allowed to mature without water and others still needed water. The cattle were some distance away in a pasture, so I rode around the herd every day. Our sheep were pastured out to rental property and as the lambs were still young, I checked them often also. My daily routine was filled, but I took time from it to go to the arena each evening. I was there for a short visit with Carla before she left for town. Regardless of how tired and dirty I was from working all day, Carla would not leave without our hug and kiss. She responded with enthusiasm; completely unlike the Carla I had known all those years.

The big County Fair horse race was only one week away, so Carla and I figured it was time to take Sapphire to the fair ground race track, so she could get familiar with her surroundings and we would be able to time her on the track where she would be racing. We were allowed on the track on Wednesday and Saturday. We loaded Sapphire into the trailer I used for hauling Nochi and drove to the tracks, with Carla following in her Volkswagon. The second time Carla rode her around the track it was apparent that we had done our job well. There was no way Billy's horse, "Trigger" could win against Sapphire. The plan was to take Sapphire to the boarding place Carla rented, leave Sapphire and the trailer there, and I would meet them at the fairground track Saturday afternoon. Kati rode in with me to watch Sapphire run the track. I promised Kati I would let her play jockey and ride Sapphire around a few laps. She was thrilled to be allowed to ride a "winner" as we jokingly referred to our Sapphire.

Kati mounted Sapphire like a pro and made the first lap around. She sat as if she had taken lessons all her life. I was really proud of my little sister. Although she is now a Junior in highschool I still refer to her as "my little sis." When she was half way around her second lap, I heard a shrill whistle; when I looked to the entrance gate, I saw "Billy the Bully" riding Trigger, heading for the track. He rode to where Carla and I stood and asked, " Who is the cute little redhead riding Sapphire?" I answered him civily, "Oh hi Billy, that cute little readhead, as you referred to her, is my sister!" "Oh yeah," he quipped,

" I sure would I like to get her to myself, I'll bet she's a hot little babe!" I was so angry at his degrading remarks about my sister I felt like popping him in the eye like I did in the store, but remembering my promise to my father, instead of hitting him, I gave him a good tongue lashing. "Listen Billy, don't ever make remarks about my sister again, and I dare you to come around her." "Oh is that so? well we'll just see about that." He gave a loud "wolf whistle and rode like the wind to catch up to Kati. I was proud of her response to the whistle; she gave Sapphire a tap with the whip and put her into a gallop. When she was back to where Carla and I stood watching, she dismounted and said, "Well he is pretty cute; more than most guys I know!" Listen Sis I muttered," I don't think you know who this guy is. I'm sure you have heard me mention "Billy the Bully" back in high school. Well, that's him. He may be tall and handsome, but he has something lacking up here." I pointed to my head. "Please, do me a favor and do not get involved with the guy. You will be sorry if you do." "I hear you Mark, but since when do I owe you a favor?" We drove home in silence; each of us engrossed in our own thoughts. Mine were on my date with Lisa later in the evening, and I can't imagine what Kati was thinking after my warning to her about Billy.

Lisa and I went to the drive-in theater to see " Rear Window," which was supposed to be one of the best movies of the year. Later we drove to a secluded area off the main highway, and once again let our passion take over. During the time I was with Lisa, Carla never entered my mind, but driving home at a much too late hour, a feeling of guilt cursed through my body. I tried to push it out of my mind, but it hung there like a cancer eating away at my soul. I loved Carla so much and had for years, but my feelings for Lisa were stronger than anything I had ever known. "Please God" I prayed, "Show me the way out of this mess. I have sinned miserably and I need your help." After my sincere prayer and the faith my parents had instilled in me I had only to wait; perhaps days, months or even years, but I knew help was coming my way.

For the first time since Father's death, my mother felt strong enough to attend church. During breakfast she asked if anyone would like to go along; expecting the usual excuses from Kati and I, but this time I said, "Yes Mother, I'll go. The roof may fall in, but I would love to go;" remembering full well my prayer, and the situation I had put myself in. Mom smiled at me and said, " No son, I don't think the roof will fall in. We will leave in about thirty minutes."

The days have flown by, and the big race is tomorrow. Carla and I are satisfied that we have done the best we could in training Sapphire, and feel that her chances of winning the race is good, but we realize also that Billy has worked Trigger very hard. Trigger and Sapphire are not the only horses entering the race hoping to win, and since we really don't know anything about the other horses we may lose the race. If that happens we will simply look forward to next year. I plan on entering Harmony in next year's race. Harmony is also a thorough-bred and chances are, she will become a winner, like her father,"Noch. After what seemed like an eternity, with the horses restless, and their jockeys trying to hold them back, the flag came down, and they were off! Billy on Trigger took the lead right away with a couple of horses from other towns running close to Trigger. Carla gave Sapphire a nudge in the flank and she sped up, but then started holding her back. The race was half over, the crowd was screaming and cheering for their favorite horse. Carla's parents and my family were surprised at how fast some horses that were strangers to our immediate area, were running. They were giving Billy a challenge he had never dreamed of, but look who is moving up. Carla was moving up! She had been deliberately holding Sapphire back, but now she was easing up on the reins, giving Sapphire the freedom to move up to her racing speed. The crowd was going wild. It was easy to see who the favorite horse was. Of course Billy had his cheering section, but Carla had been very popular and highly regarded during her years in school, even having the honor of being Valedictorian of her class. Sapphire was moving up, but two other horses were still in the lead. "Big Joe" a horse from Lovell, a very small town about twenty five miles away, had won two races in the past and was also favored. Big Joe was running neck to neck with Trigger, but Sapphire continued to gain on them. She was running with a determination that exceeded all expectations. All the while, Carla was leaning forward talking to Sapphire coaxing her on. As I watched I was also saying, "Come

on Sapphire, you can do it, go you're all most there!" I
wanted Sapphire to win the race, but my heart was in it
for Carla. Sapphire was now side by side with Big Joe
and Trigger. I could see the flagman holding the flag
up, looking at his timer. Carla was head to head with
Billy. She gave Sapphire a final nudge in the flank; the
flag came down, I opened my eyes, Carla and Sapphire
had won by a nose! They continued down the stretch
a bit further, giving Sapphire time to slow down and
Carla time to breathe. The three judges were waiting
to congratulate the jockey, and presented her with a
beautiful array of roses. She held the roses in one arm,
patted Sapphire lovingly and blew a kiss to her parents
and me, and my family. People gathered around Billy to
congratulate him on the good race he ran, but he was
clearly uneasy and upset. For once in his life, he had lost
to two girls; Carla and Sapphire. As I walked past him
on my way to help Carla load Sapphire in the trailer, I
overheard him say, "That little hussy will never beat me
again; I'll make sure of that!" His remark upset me, as I
would not be surprised at anything terrible he planned
to do. My imagination kicked in and I could think of
all the trouble he could do to my family. He knew how
much I cared for Carla, and I suspected his meanness
would be directed at me. He would stop at nothing to
get back at Carla and me.

The race was over; Carla was still receiving calls
and cards congratulating her on the big win. The next
step was the Montana State Fair in Billings. The purse
for the Billings race was much larger; mostly because

people could place bets, often placing large amounts on their favorite horse. The Montana race also drew more entries which made competition a greater challenge. The Billings race was a long time dream for Carla and me, but first we had to win the county before we could enter the big Montana race. Now that we had won the county, we were looking forward to fulfilling our dream.

After the horses were safely loaded into the trailer, we now had to decide where they would live. Carla spoke up immediately and asked, "Mark, please be honest, and give me a truthful answer. How do you feel about keeping Sapphire and Harmony at your place?" I shook my head like a "No, No, then laughed, "How do you think I feel, Carla? I was hoping you would ask. Katie and I would be lost without horses around, so the answer is yes. I"m not ready to buy another horse to ride and I would not know how to spend my free time if I couldn't ride." Carla was so happy, I wanted to take her to dinner or go dancing; she loved to dance, but I was still dating Lisa on Saturday night, and the rush I felt when I thought of our date kept me from ending or postponing our relationship.

Carla and I unloaded the horses and made a riding date for Sunday afternoon. A love of riding was our favorite time together. Tonight I will be with Lisa, then Sunday afternoon, I will be spending time with Carla. My life is really messed up. If I had a problem that I needed help with or someone to talk to, I always went to my father who listened. Although I am an adult, starting my second year in college I need a good ear to listen and advise. This is the first time since he died that I needed to reach out to him, but he is not here and I miss him; my dad was my best friend. I remember something he always said to me, and that was, "take your time son," he cautioned, "important decisions take time. Often problems work themselves out. God doesn't answer our prayers overnight." Dad is helping me through my memories of the many times we had serious conversations. This time my problem was loving two girls in different ways" Sometime in the near future I would have to choose, because my conscience would force me to.

My date with Lisa last night was great. We exchanged jokes, laughed a lot, and talked about serious things, such as the coming college year. She asked questions about the ranch, and seemed to know much more than I realized about farm life. We drove to the cafe and bus depot to meet her parents, who were pleased to finally meet "her guy" as she referred to me. They offered to serve us dinner, which we did not accept. We drove to her house, about one block from the cafe. She unlocked the door, put her arms around my neck, but instead of a goodnight kiss, she whispered, "we aren't through yet, are we Mark?"

Chapter 13
THE SNAKE BITE

ARLA AND I rode Sapphire and Harmony down the trail to the creek and the old oak tree. Carla wanted to ride Harmony, so she could have the pleasure of riding a newly broken future race horse. Of course I mounted Sapphire, the winner, as we lovingly referred to her. Carla was leaving for College in one week, and I needed to know how she felt about our relationship. Did she still think going steady was a bad idea, or was it now time for the commitment I longed for almost a year ago. Until I met Lisa, I knew I wanted Carla for my life partner. But now I also have strong feelings for Lisa. As we rode along in silence, I looked up to Heart Mountain. The sun was dropping behind the mountain, and it appeared to be a large red ball, slowly hiding its face behind the majestic shadowy mountain. Even at the young age of ten or twelve I loved to watch this same sun dropping behind Heart Mountain and a feeling of protection came over me. Carla broke my spell when she said, "you're very quiet Mark, I'll give you a penny for your thoughts!" "Sorry, Carla, I guess I was caught up in daydreaming, when I should have been paying attention to my favorite girl; and I don't mean Sapphire!" She smiled and put Harmony into a trot. I followed her to the corral.

When I stepped into the living room, I over heard Mom and Kati having a serious conversation, "but Mother," Kati said, " Billy is the cutest guy, and he treats me great." Then Mom argued, "I know darling. It's just that you came home later than ever before, and I was worried. I hope that doesn't happen again. I know very little about Billy, except he has a questionable reputation, and he did keep you out late." Kati did not answer, but turned and went to her room. I didn't want Mother to know I was eavesdropping, but thought to myself, "so soon after the race? He's beginning to get his revenge already." Billy is well aware that nothing could hurt me more than having my little sister involved with him, and even more to have a love relationship with him. He has never come to the ranch to pick her up, so she is meeting him in town. I will talk to her if she continues to go out with my worst enemy. He is still "Billy the Bully" to me as he was in high school. He was certain his Trigger would win the fair race, but Sapphire won with Carla as the jockey; he will harbor his anger and disappointment until he is satisfied with the revenge he heaps upon me and those close to me, and will stop at nothing to get it.

Tony and I were busy irrigating some fields that were not ready to harvest, when I heard Tony yell, "Help!" He was about three hundred yards down the field away from me. He was waving his arms and yelling, "my boy is hurt! Snakebite, snakebite, help." I started running toward him, when I heard the word, "snakebite" Tony's eight year old son, Jose was following his father, not looking to the ground and the snake was coiled ready to strike when Jose stepped on it. He screamed and started running toward his father. Running is a "no no" if you have a snakebite, as it increases blood circulation and the venom spreads through the body much faster. Jose was still screaming when his papa reached him. He gathered his son in his arms and, with me close behind, we headed for my truck. On our way to the car, I caught a glimpse of the rattler crawling away. I did not take time to kill the snake, and besides I dropped my shovel when I heard Tony yelling for me and had nothing to kill it with, but was able to recognize it as a "diamond-back rattler" People have been known to die from this kind of snakebite, if they do not receive treatment soon after the bite. I drove as fast as I dared, but by the time we reached the hospital, carried the boy in and called for a Doctor an hour had passed. Jose was dropping in and out of consciencness. Time is essential, and I was worried that too much time had gone by since the bite. The bite from a diamond-back rattler takes priority over other emergencies, so he was taken immediately to the emergency room for treatment shortly after we rushed in the door. Tony was beside himself with worry. Jose was his only son. He had two girls, but it was obvious that he took special pride in his boy. Tony had worked for us several years, and my family had become quite fond of his wife and children. I was praying with all my heart that Jose would survive the awful snakebite.

When the Doctor came to report on Jose's condition, I could see deep concern in his expression. he hesitated, looked at me and continued, "The boy is still unconscious, we are doing all we can, but blood circulates much faster through the body in children than in an adult, so I am afraid that running away from the snake to where you were, as you said he did, may have caused the venom to travel through his body much too fast. We will continue working with him and hopefully we can save him." He looked at me and said,"you may want to get the boy's mother in to the hospital soon." Tony was sitting quietly holding his head down propped with his hands. I knew he was praying for his son's life. The family are faithful Catholics, and no matter how busy we are on the ranch, Tony takes enough time off on Sunday to attend Mass with his wife and children.

When I reached the ranch, I went directly to Tony's house and gave Maria the bad news about her son being bitten by a snake, and told her I would drive her to the hospital as soon as I checked the irrigation water, then I went to the field where I had been irrigating, only to find the water was completely out of control. It was running in every direction except the rows where was meant to be. I managed to reset the water to run down the rows, then checked the field where Tony was working when he heard Jose yelling "snake, snake! papa, snake!" Jose was in second grade in school and was learning to speak English, so he spoke Spanish part time, and English other times, depending on to whom he was speaking. When I honked the horn for my passenger, she came immediately and we were on our way to the hospital, so she could be with her son. Of course Tony needed her support also. Both Tony and Maria were allowed to sit beside their son, hoping any minute he would open his eyes, but Jose remained in a coma. He was receiving medication intravenously, and also was being kept on oxygen to aid him with breathing.

I asked Maria if I should take the other two children home with me, but she had called her sister, who lived and worked on a farm about five miles away, to pick up the two little girls, and take care of them until she returned. It was a sad picture I carried in my mind and heart as I drove back to the ranch to finish irrigating the fields Tony and I left unfinished.

When I walked into the kitchen, Mother was busy at the sink washing vegetables from the garden, and Kati was getting the dishes and silverware on the table for our evening meal. They looked up from their chores, and could tell by the look on my face that something was wrong. "Whats up Mark?" Kati asked, giving me one of her impish smiles. "Did you lose a baby calf? Or worse yet, heaven forbid, a horse got his tail caught in the gate?" She stopped joking and said, "seriously Mark what is wrong? You are as pale as a sheet." When I told them about the snake biting Jose, and that he remained in a

coma, all smiles and jokes went away, and I was flooded
with questions, about when and where it happened. I
told them about how Jose had run to his father, which
was at least one hundred yards, they spoke up at the
same time, "Oh no, he never should have run." Mother
said, "I've always known that the best thing to do if a
person gets a snakebite, is to stay as still as possible, to
keep the blood from circulating through the body. But
he is just a little boy, and didn't know what to do except
run for his Dad. I wish there was something I could do
to help. We will drive in this evening and ask if they
need me to do anything for them or the girls." Upon
our arrival at the hospital, we were given permission to
go directly to Jose's room. When Maria saw us enter
the door, she came to me, and fell into my arms. I held
her fast, tried to wipe the tears from her face, conforted
her as much as possible, and finally crossed the room to
where Tony stood motionless, but looked up and gave
a sign of greeting. Tony said to Mother in his broken
English, "I'm glad you are here. The Doctors say he is
no better," then he broke into tears. "We need a priest,
Mrs. Masters, if you can get us one. "Of course, I'll call
right-away. Now is there anything else we can do?

The funeral for Jose was a simple one, with only a few
relatives, as most of their family was still in Mexico. Some
neighbors and friends, Jose's teacher, and the principle
of the school attended. A few ladies from their church
hosted a luncheon in the dining room of the church.
Although we go to a different church, Mother and Kati
furnished food and helped the ladies with the luncheon.

Chapter 14
HARMONY MISSING

BEFORE WE saddled Sapphire and Harmony up for our last ride before Carla left for college, she wanted to deliver a gift and condolences to Tony and Maria, whom she had become friends with during the many years she had been coming to the ranch. She and her parents gave them a lovely card with a fifty dollar gift certificate to J.C. Penny store, where her father was manager. She asked Maria to not open the card until the family were all home. Maria thanked her graciously in Spanish, stepped forward and gave Carla a big hug, then laughingly gave me a hug saying in her broken English, "and Mr. Mark, you deserve a hug too."

Carla and I rode for hours, first around the neighboring farms, commenting on various things we noticed along the way; animals, crops, new homes etc; Finally, we went to our favorite spot by the creek where the big oak stood tall and stalwart; It's heavy limbs full of leaves spreading in every direction offering a resting place for a couple of riders to dismount. We led Sapphire and Harmony to the creek for a drink, then let them munch away on the grass. Horses never get so full of food that they can't graze.

We sat side by side on a large limb that had fallen from the oak sometime in the past; no doubt it fell during one of the strong winds Wyoming is famous for. There is an old saying that goes, "silence is golden" and if the saying is true, both Carla and I were cherishing our last time together in silence. She would not be back until Christmas vacation, almost four months away. We both started to speak at once, then she said, "me first, Mark. I have had a lot of time to think about our friendship and, our relationship; and where it might lead us. One thing I know for sure is I will never be happy without you in my life." I had longed to hear those words for two years, but now with Lisa in my life, and the guilt I had about my relationship with her, left me at a total loss for a reply to Carla's sincere words. I wanted her know I felt the way she did about facing life without her, yet, how can I do this? Without saying a word, I stood, took both her hands in mine and pulled her up close. I could see the love she had for me in her eyes, so full of compassion, understanding and faithfulness. When we kissed, the passion we shared was a dream come true. Carla was completely submissive, leaning her body into mine until it seemed nothing would stop us from making love, then suddenly she pulled away

and said, "no Mark, let's stop this now. I promised my
parents and myself that I would be a virgin until my
wedding night. I am sorry if you are disappointed, but I
will not break that promise." I gathered her in my arms
again, and spoke softly. "Carla, I love you so much, and
I admire you more than you will ever realize for your
decision. If I was a bit disappointed, it will pass, but
always remember my love for you will   grow every day,
until we are together again.

Carla and I parted with me implicitly returning her
love, but with no commitment. The strong confession
she had made of her love for me along with her hopes
and dreams for the future, certainly deserved more
than I was able to give. She drove away; off to college
never dreaming that she planned to spend her life with
an unfaithful idiot, who doesn't have the backbone to
make a serious decision.

Carla and her parents will drive to Montana
tomorrow, Sunday. They plan to get her settled in
an affordable apartment, near the college if possible.
They are proud of their daughter as they have a right
to be. She is an excellent student, with certain goals
for her life, and above all her morals are impeccable.
She demonstrated that today when we were together;
another reason to love her as I do.

Two weeks have passed since Lisa and I had a date.
I miss her smile, our light-hearted conversations, but
most of all I miss the closeness of our bodies. As the
time draws near for our date tonight, the urge to be

with her is so strong I cannot imagine never being with her again. Is this a fascination or is it true love?

Lisa saw my truck pull up in her grandmothers driveway, and greeted me at the door without waiting for me to ring the doorbell. "Oh Mark, I thought you would never get here. Hey, you look great! What have you been up to lately?" Without answering her, I put my arms out and she fell into them. I was hungry for her kisses, and returned them eagerly. "My grandmother will be back from shopping in an hour," she said, "please come in Mark, it's been so long, much too long. please promise you will never stay away that long again, please!" Before I could make that promise, we were in the bedroom with the door closed.

While driving home, I prayed, "Oh God, I am so weak and vulnerable, please show me the way. I cannot do it without your help. I love Carla so much, but this urge I have to be with Lisa takes over my mind and body. I really do need help!"

Most of our crops were harvested and a great deal of the pressure was off my shoulders. Tony, with detailed instructions from me, along with his two helpers could take care of the field work. I was free at last to get Sapphire and Kati ready for the Montana State Fair horse race. We were winners in Park County, which entitled us to enter the big race coming soon. Kati had never been a jockey in a race and needed all the training we could give her within the short time left until the big day.

My college classes will begin next week, and of course Kati was already in school, so our riding sessions will have to be after she gets home from school and week-ends. Kati would grab a snack, change her clothes, and head for the corral. "Okay Kati, it's now or never; the time has come to get serious, if you still want to ride Sapphire in the Billings race" "Oh, I do. Mark, I've been waiting for you to get caught up with the harvest, so we can practice. I promise I'll do my best." "Thats great, Kati, I'm glad to hear you say that, so we will begin tomorrow, okay? I looked at Mom and she was smiling. "Whats up Mom, why the unusually big smile?" She took a sip of her coffee, and said, "I was just happy to see you two getting along so well; I hope you keep it up."

Kati was elated when she was chosen to ride Sapphire in a race, especially the "big race" as it was referred to in our part of the country. She had watched Carla mount Sapphire many times, and tried to mimic Carla in as many ways as she could remember. When Kati mounted Sapphire, it was like watching Carla all over again. I was very impressed with the way she sat, and especially when she changed from and easy gait to one considerably faster. I complimented her as much as I could without building up that; already inflated ego she had. Since Kati was a little girl, she was complimented on her beautiful red hair and blue eyes, and she began to think it was true. Our father presented her as his little red head angel, and Mother called her my beautiful baby, but I referred to her as "my bratty little sister." I asked myself, "can I possibly be her jealous big brother?" She is a senior now, and I am a college student; surely she and I have matured, and become sensible adults; Kati is no longer my "bratty little sister, and I must try to get such a childish idea out of my head. When she calls to me asking, "Mark, how am I doing with this jockey business?" I will say, "Hey sis, you are doing great! Much better than I ever expected you could. Keep it up, Kati, keep it up!" She took my advice to "keep it up," and in only a few days, my sister looked as good on Sapphire as Carla did when she raced. I will be proud to enter her and Sapphire in the big race. Carla's parents will drive to Billings to watch Sapphire race, and they have informed me that they are flying Carla to Billings for the race. Of course it will be an excuse to see their daughter. My mother will also be on hand to watch Kati perform, so we will have a nice little cheering section in the grandstand.

I had finished watering the animals, and making sure all gates were fastened to prevent the wind from blowing them open during the night, when I saw Billy's truck turn in the driveway. He stepped out, waved to me and called out, "Hey farmer boy, how's it going?" Visions of trouble immediately loomed through my mind. What could this character possibly have in his mind that would bring him all the way from town to our ranch? I answered him civilly, even though he greeted me with the two words I really resented being called. In the first place I am no longer a young boy. as I was when he first called me, farmer boy, and secondly

I am a rancher. I waved back to him saying, "hey city boy, the question is, aren't you lost, so far from town. What gives?" When he answered me with a shrug of the shoulders, "I thought I would take a look at those horses you are so proud of, and hopefully get to watch that good looking sister of yours ride around the arena a few times. She's quite a gal, that girl!" What a nerve this guy had. My patience was running out, but I remained calm and said, " Yeah Billy, she is good looking, but remember, she is my sister and I'll do whatever it takes to protect her from guys like you, I'm warning you Billy, stay away from Kati!" I drove away and left him sitting in his car, blowing his horn like a maniac, trying to upset me more than he already had. Now it was time to have a serious talk with Kati about this guy. With the race .only three days away, I decided to wait until after the race to deal with Kati. After overhearing a conversation between Mom and Kati about her dating Billy, I had a feeling that the subject would not be a pleasant one. I do not want to do anything that might cause her to do less than her best in the race. When the race is over, I will confront her on dating someone as vindictive as I know Billy to be. What a race this one was! Kati did a beautiful job of controlling Sapphire; I could not have ask for a better job. She remembered all the things we worked on during our training sessions, but there were several horses that were faster than Sapphire, so she came out in third place, and received five hundred dollars as prize money. She will, of course give Carla her share, although I doubt that Carla will accept it. Just like a girl, she talked Mom into taking her shopping before they left Billings for the return trip home.

Even though I was towing my horse trailer with Sapphire as a passenger, the temptation to go to Lisa's home was so strong I could not resist seeing her. I told myself, I would only stay a few minutes, but the time passed and I was there at least an hour. We were thrilled to be together again. Mom and Kati were watching a show on telivision and I knew I would have some explaining to do, so I gave each of them a hug and rushed off to bed with the excuse that I was exhausted from the days activities and needed some rest. Even so, I saw questioning expressions on their faces.

When I woke this morning, and peeked out the window, I was greeted by a stormy day. I knew the wind was blowing, but was surprised to see that a thin layer of snow had fallen during the night. Considering the stormy weather, and the fact that Tony had done the chores last evening I decided to have breakfast before going to the corral. I reminded Tony to make certain the gates were securely fastened, and trusted him in every way to do his best, so I figured things were okay at the corral. Also I was looking forward to Mother's Sunday morning breakfast of sausage and pancakes. Our family has always had a tradition of everyone gathering for breakfast on Sunday mornings. We discussed the things we had done the past week and plans for the coming week. We have kept this up, even though Father is not with us anymore. There are only three of us now, but we still enjoy our Sunday morning breakfasts. When breakfast was over, I dressed in a warm hooded jacket and faced the outside world; cold winds and flakes of snow were falling, even though it was only the last week of September. Summers are short in Wyoming; old man winter can't wait to get started pounding our valley with his strong cold winds, that drive aninals to shelter, and Wyomites to drag out their heavy clothing. Winter weather that appears in September, seldom stays, but gives us a good sample of what is to come. After the first small storm, autumn comes along with bright sunny warm days. Many citizens consider autumn to be the best of all seasons, as the harvest is over, and it is time to relax before our real winter comes. I drove in the barnyard, and suddenly had a feeling that something was wrong. I looked in the direction of the horse shed and saw the door was open, then realized the horses were not in the corral or shed. I was stunned; where in heavens name were Sapphire and Harmony? I ran to the other side of the barn, looked all around, then focused on the nearby fields. I spotted Sapphire in the distance, but no Harmony. I ran to get a bridle, so I could catch Sapphire. A least I found Sapphire. Thank goodness for that, but Harmony was nowhere in sight. I ran and walked down the field to where Sapphire was grazing contentedly on some stubble in a hay field. I slowed down, walked carefully to where she stood and placed the bridle on. Now I could ride her back to the corral.When I reached the corral, I removed the bridle and hurriedly drove home to get Kati's help. She rode

Sapphire and I drove my truck. We searched for hours, with no luck. Whoever turned the horses out, had given Harmony a big slap on the rump and caused her to run away. After giving up finding her within our own area, we came back to the corral. Kati called me,"Hey Mark, come look at this." She pointed to some strange car tracks. They did not belong to my car and certainly not to Tony's old pickup truck that we furnished him for driving around the ranch. At once, I recognized them as being the kind I had noticed on Billy's truck. They were big wide tracks; the kind of treads that are supposed to be cool, and the kind all guys in his crowd use on their cars. That's it Kati I said, "Billy came sometime last night and turned our horses out." He is very angry with me; I"ll explain when we get home. "Yes sir Kati, Billy the Bully is the culprit. We will be lucky if we ever see Harmony again!" Mom was as anxious as Kati and I. When we broke the bad news she said, "You kids know how badly I feel about Harmony. and I will do everything I can to help find her. I do have a suggestion. I will make signs describing Harmony and we will put them out on telephone poles and etc; so people will be watching for her. Kati and I will use my car tomorrow, and drive this whole area; she must be somewhere, unless a person needing a horse has her hidden away in a barn." When she said that, I really panicked. She was right, we might never find her. At this point Kati began to cry. Mom handed her a tissue, and tried to console her by saying, "Kati darling, we'll get another horse. It may not be a thoroughbred like

Harmony but, we'll get a good saddle horse for you."
When I witnessed the litle scene between Mom and
Kati, I thought, "why is my sister so upset? Harmony
belonged to me, seems like I should be the one crying."
Mom followed through with her promise to make signs,
which we posted over the entire area. The signs read:
LOST in large letters across the top, then below it gave
a description of Harmony. "Black Mare two years old
with white spot on left lower leg. If you see this horse,
please call 801-373-0203." I placed the advertisement
in our local newspaper, hoping someone would read it
and see our horse, but with no luck. I took pictures of
the strange tracks we saw in the barn yard driveway to
have as evidence, and showed them to the sheriff. He
was a long time friend to my dad when he was alive,
and of course had heard about my Nochi winning the
county race a few years back. He was surprised to hear
about Sapphire winning at the Park County race, then
entering the race in Montana Being a racing fan, he
felt badly about Harmony's disappearance. He looked at
the pictures of the tire tracks and agreed that my horse
could have been stolen, possibly walked or ridden to a
parked trailer nearby. "I'll tell you what I'll do Mark,
I will see if I can match these tracks to any of those
hoodlums that hang out around here that have the wide
tires on their cars. If you know any of those fellows,
tell me now; it may save us a lot of time." I had not
planned on mentioning the one person that I had in
mind, but he asked me, so I gave him Billy's name, and
mentioned that I had gotten threatening remarks from

Billy. "Oh hey," he said, "I know that guy. I've written him up a couple of times for speeding. Well, once for speeding and another time he actually ran the one red light we have in this town. Yeah, I'll check him out! If that horse of yours hads been stolen, we'll find the thief." I thanked him for his help; feeling like a load had been lifted as we now had professional help to find Harmony. I rushed home to tell Mom and Kati about my visit with the Sherrif. Of course, Kati didn't believe that a nice guy like Billy would steal. Especially the horse that she loved so much! Mother found it hard to believe that Harmony had been stolen, rather than ran away as we first thought, but agreed it was a possibility. I decided, after about a week, to call Carla with the news of Harmony's disappearance. When she answered the phone, and heard my voice she said, "Mark, it's so good to hear your voice, but tell me, what's wrong? You never call unless you have something special to tell me. What is it?" "Carla, I said, "Harmony is missing. She ran away, or maybe she was stolen." There was a long silence, so long that I said, "Carla, are you still there?" She answered, " Yes Mark, I'm still here. You know me, I cry at the "drop of a hat". I know you are doing everything in your power to find her. I wish I was there to help. Please call me, again when you get some news. I know calling long distance is expensive, but Mark, I miss hearing your voice. Sometimes I wish I had stayed home to go to college, but I made the decision, and now I have to live with it. I try to think positive about being away from you. " Carla" I said, you know how much I miss you, but it won't be long until Christmas." We said our goodbyes and hung up.

Time was flying by; it had been a month since Harmony so mysteriously disappeared. I was keeping in touch with the sheriff, checking for news of my horse. This time he did have a bit of news to report. "Yes, Mark, I followed some of the guys that use the wide tires; comparing each tire with the picture you took, and found an interesting clue. All the tires I checked were about the same age. These boys had agreed to buy the wide tires about the same time, but one truck had a new tire. The new tire had heavier treads than all the others, and it was the one that bore down through the snow and mud, leaving a visible track. I can't say who that truck belongs to until I dig up a bit more evidence." I thanked him for his effort and replied, "Sounds like we may be a little closer, Sheriff. I can't thank you enough for your interest and time with this horse deal."

We had finished dinner, and I was clearing the table; as my trade with Kati called for, "dishes for typing" when the phone rang. I answered, and a voice said,

" is this 307-754-3065? "Yes it is; what can I do for you?" He hesitated, then began explaining the reason for his call. "Well Mr....." I interrupted, "call me Mark Sir," "Okay thanks Mark, I live on a ranch in Meteetse; I'm sure you have

heard of Meteetse, so anyway, I purchased a horse from a guy that was driving through town on his way to Cheyenne WY, and apparently needed some cash. His story sounded convincing, and the price was right, so I bought the horse, and took it home for my daughter to ride. I was back in town the following day and saw your sign at the post office where we get our mail. When I saw the sign, I knew right away I had made a big mistake. I had been ripped off. The sign in the post office gave the very same description; black, white spot on left foot. Looks like the same horse I paid two hundred dollars for. I wrote the number down, and decided to call this number. "Mark, do you suppose I got filched and bought a stolen horse?" I did not want to sound too sure, so said, "it's entirely possible. If you will give me directions, I will come take a look. I will recognize my horse at a glance." I wrote the directions to his ranch down, and told him I would be down early Saturday morning. When I returned home with the news, Mom suggested I take the sheriff along in hopes we might gather a few more details. She and I felt sure we knew who had taken Harmony. Even Kati agreed that Billy might be responsible. Now what we assumed was a lost horse was looking very much like a theft.

When the sheriff and I arrived at the ranch where Harmony had been taken, my heart sunk when I saw her. She looked as if she had not been fed in weeks. her hip bones stood out from the weight she had lost, she was dirty and unkempt . Tears came to my eyes when I saw my horse in this terrible shape. I understand why the rancher had paid only two hundred dollars for her. I'm sure he planned to take her home, feed her, brush her mane and tail and she would be a fine horse.

I paid the man the two hundred dollars he had invested, plus an extra fifty for being so honest and helpful. The sheriff and I both thanked him profusely for the help he had given us. I drove home with a happy heart. Sheriff Sam promised to stay with the clues and information he had gathered the past two weeks until he found the horse thief. We both had strong suspicions that Billy was our man, but needed some concrete evidence before he could arrest him. It took only three days for the sheriff to get his "cards stacked" and arrest Billy for stealing Harmony. What a fool Billy was to think he could get by with the theft. After a few days in jail, he admitted to stealing Harmony. Billy told the sheriff that he never suspected that our "Horse Lost" signs would reach far out places like Meteetse, or that anyone would take pictures of his tire tracks and compare them to the ones on his truck. Billy now sits in jail in Cody, Wyoming waiting for his trial in court. Billy promised that he would do something to hurt me, when I told him to stay away from my sister. He kept his word, and I must say he did a good job of it.

He not only got back at me in a big way, but lost Kati's interest in him. I came out the winner; I not only have my horse back, but Kati will no longer be dating Billy.

Chapter 15
THE BREAKUP

NOVEMBER CAME and went with no major storms crossing our valley, just the usual cold dry winds. When I set my gaze on Heart Mountain, I never bcame tired of its beauty and splendor, but that too can change. Often in a matter of minutes, it may take on a dark angry look which warns people in this valley to get ready. A blizzard is coming. Occasionally, the storm loses its strength and only brings on a few flurries, but often we are faced with fierce winds, snow drifts, and freezing temperatures. Schools close, as school busses are unable to transport students, due to many roads being impassable. When I look at Heart Mountain and I see a cloudy face I take notice. I checked the water heater in the barn, making sure water did not freeze, gave the animals extra feed, took special care that gates were locked securely against the wind.

When I stepped in the rear door, and removed my boots, I was greeted with the delicious smell of food cooking. "What's cooking, Mom?" Kati said, "Don't tell him Mom, if he can't recognize it by the smell, he doesn' get any." "Okay Kati," I quipped. " just because your boy friend is in jail, you don't need to be so mean to me. After all I got your horse back, didn't I? She did her Katie thing, and stuck her tongue at me, but laughingly said, "You know very well, I almost hate the guy now, so there, "put that in your pipe and smoke it, Mr. smart guy!"

Carla would be home in two weeks for the Christmas holidays. I could hardly wait to see her again and promised myself to spend as much time as possible with her. When we were together I felt at peace; I needed to share my life with her, and wanted to be a part of hers. The only thing I could not share with her was my affair with Lisa. I continued to be with Lisa every Saturday, but as time passed, I began to realize my feelings for her were not, and never had been love. From the beginning of our relationship, we were physically attracted, but love and marriage were not a part of it. Lisa was cute, fun to go out with and certainly not one bit intimidated about acting on her sexual feelings. There is no doubt in my mind that she would be sharing those feelings with someone else soon after we are no longer dating. I often wonder how I could have been so blind for so long; allowing the desires of my body to consume my thinking and actions. a My prayers were being answered, but I wasn' t listening; I am listening now!

When Lisa came to the door she fell into my arms as usual. I held her tight, returning her kisses, but reminding myself, "This is the time to listen to a voice in my head that kept saying, "Don't do this! Are you listening?" I dropped my arms from around her, the kisses stopped and I said, "Lisa, we need to talk." She stepped back and asked, "Mark what's this all about, have you gone mad?" I suggested we go inside I took her hand, and led her to the couch. By this time, I could see the shock, and questioning expression on her face. "Lisa, I have something to tell you. I should have told you months ago, but I enjoyed our dates so much, I couldn't bring myself to stop coming. I think you know what I mean." "Mark, are you breaking up with me?" I saw the tears coming to her eyes, and she began to cry. "Why Mark, why?" I handed her my handkerchief to wipe the tears; all the time telling myself not to be weak. My mind was made up and I must not give in to those tears. The thought continued to cross my mind, "are you listening, are you listening?" I told Lisa the entire story. How I had loved Carla for many years, but considered it a strong friendship, until the last time she was home, we exchanged the true love we had for each other. I told her about Carla's vow to herself, and her parents to remain a virgin until marriage, and that I agreed to honor that vow along with her. "It is true love, lasting love, and will lead to marriage. These are the reasons we cannot be together again. I am truly sorry to have hurt you, but am sure you will find a new boy friend soon." What I saw on her face were shock, anger, unbelief and hurt. Through another flood of tears, she looked at me and said, "Yes Mark, I'm sure I will. See ya around." Without looking back, she closed the door. I went to my car, drove home and for once in a long time was rid of the guilt I had felt for so long.

Chapter 16
MOUNTAINS

ONE WEEK after Christmas vacation until finals, and then only four months until I will graduate from the two year community college here within driving distance of this ranch; where I plan to spend my life, just as my parents have done. Never a day goes by that I don' t look toward 'my mountain' as I refer to "Heart Mountain" and gain courage to face life with renewed strength, as I did when my father was suddenly taken from me and my family. I have been reading through a new book I found recently in the college library that suggests there are "mountains behind mountains." These mountains can be fear, financial struggles, an addiction, death of a loved one. Any number of mountains may occur in life, but when I gaze at "my mountain" and realize how it has withstood the adversities of nature through the ages, I am reminded that the same creator that made that mountain, also made me, and I too can face my mountains with the same strength as I see on the face of Heart mountain.

When Carla comes home from school for Christmas vacation we will spend many hours together, riding, catching up on happenings during our months apart and perhaps making some plans for the future.

Our first Christmas without my father will be a challenge for Mother, Kati and me, but we agreed at dinner last evening that we could and would carry on as if he was with us. Of course things will be different in many ways, so we must accept the change and try to carry on. Shopping has already begun with Mom and Kati and as usual my shopping will be last minute. Kati and I plan to go to the same spot where we went with our Dad to choose a tree, drag it down the mountain to our truck, set it up in the living room, and congratulate ourselves for getting the most beautiful tree in the forest! Later, Mother and Kati will bring out decorations, including some ornaments saved from childhood days. Always remembering Father and his part in all this, but not giving in to grief. When we discussed how we would handle Christmas without a husband and father, Kati reminded us that by Carrying on as we planned we would be making Father proud of the little family he left behind.

Carla arrived home today, just ahead of a storm that was bringing cold winds and snow from the far north to our valley and as predicted on the news weather forecast, would make its way across the mountains south to Colorado. Although the storm carries heavy snows, the wind that causes blizzard conditions in Wyoming will diminish as the storm travels south, leaving places like Denver, Colorado with a blanket of white; enjoyable to the eye, and a playground for kids.

I had looked forward to Carla's coming home for three months, and I wasn't about to let a blizzard keep me from seeing her. After finishing chores, I changed into clean casuals, told Mom that I would not be home for dinner, and explained that I was going to see Carla. When I rang the doorbell, her Mother answered the door. She was pleased to see me and ask me to come in. She was about to call, "Carla Mark is here," but I said softly, "Don't call, I want to revved her!" She went along with the surprise, and called, "Carla, please come here, I need you!" Carla said, "Okay Mom, coming." Mrs. Nelson whispered, "I'll go now and you two can get acquainted." And we did! Carla screamed, "Mark, oh Mark!" She ran into my waiting arms. We talked about my graduation from Community College, how Sapphire and Harmony were doing, also how we planned to spend Christmas. I broke into our conversation with, "Carla, I hate to cut this short, but there is a storm brewing out there, and I really need to beat that storm home, so I'd better go now. We can talk on the phone, and make more plans. Tony and Maria are in Mexico visiting family, so I am responsible for his work and mine too." We kissed goodbye and I went out into a dark windy snowy night, hoping 'lady luck' would step in, and get me home without any problems. Blowing snow made driving hazardous, and I dreaded turning off the highway toward the ranch. Snow plows would make a few trips down the main highway between the two towns where people commuted to jobs or business, but they rarely came to the ranch roads until after all highways were cleared. Quite often a rancher used a tractor to clear snow drifts in his own area, so it was ' to each his own' when snow drifts piled up.

I turned off the main highway onto the road that led to our ranch and immediately faced more snow blowing on to my windshield. Driving was slow and hazardous, as my windshield fogged over faster than the wipers could clear it. I was determined to get home. When I finally reached the drive to our house, I drove into a snowdrift that stopped me. I could have backed up a bit, but that would not lead me closer home. I raced the motor and spun my wheels, but the truck would not move. I was stuck. I left the truck and walked the two block distance home. I was thankful that the weather was not sub-zero as it was the last time I was stuck in a snow drift, and my neighbor Abe saved my life.

I was changing to dry clothing, when I heard the wind blowing. I thought, "Nuts, why can't we have one day without another blizzard hitting." I called down to Kati and Mom, "Do you hear what I hear? The wind is bringing us another storm!" Kati called back and said, "That is a Chinook wind, silly. It's melting the snow." Chinooks provide a welcome respite from a long winter chill. These Chinook winds blow in from the eastern slopes of the Rockies.

There is a legend that came from the Yakima Indians that once there were five brothers that lived on Great

River. They were the Chinook brothers and they caused the warm wind to blow down from the Rockies, so the warm wind is called a Chinook. I was overjoyed to hear the whistling of a Chinook. It meant the snow would be gone and Carla and I could ride again .

The week passed much too quickly, and it was time for Carla to return to college. She came every day for our time together; sometimes riding or grooming the horses, but often we spent the time after a long ride, in the living room of my house, sharing ideas, and planning for the future. We both knew what our ambitions and goals were, but there was something lacking. We were sitting on the couch holding hands, when suddenly I realized what was missing; we had yet to discuss a commitment. I figured a year had passed, we both had matured, we each would soon have two years of college, and had certainly expressed our feelings about life without one another, but never a solid promise to be faithful to each other. Carla was ready to make that commitment last year when she was home, but I was dating Lisa, and my personal relationship with her was so strong in my mind and body that I could not force myself to end it. The guilt of that time in my life is still with me and no doubt will be in my thoughts until I have the nerve to confess the affair to Carla. The question is, shall I do it now or wait until much later, maybe sometime after we are married? Once again, I will take the plunge and ask Carla to become engaged, and hope my guardian angel will be with me in this big personal problem."

Chapter 17
PLANE CRASH

CARLA AND I attended a Christmas dance during her vacation from school, took in a couple of movies, drove to nearby Cody for dinner, in fact enjoyed some great times, and of course our long horse back rides. At the end of each date, we shared some kisses that told me the true love Carla and I felt for each other led to a passion far beyond what I had for Lisa. My feelings for Carla were deeply rooted and very sincere.

We saddled Sapphire and Harmony up for our last ride before Carla and her parents left for Montana. Her parents planned to continue on from Montana to south Texas for a two week visit with her grandparents who chose to spend the cold Wyoming winters in the warm climate that exists in south Texas.

Sapphire and Harmony were feeling their 'oats' as the old saying goes. They wanted to get out of the arena, and be on the way to that green stubble they grazed on every day. The weather was perfect; not hot, not cold. As we rode we played along with the extra energy they seemed to have; letting them trot and even gallop to our favorite resting place. One could not have asked for a more beautiful place to propose to, 'pop the question' as we so often hear when referring to marriage. We dismounted, staked the horses to a fallen tree limb where there was plenty of grass, and headed for the large log where we usually sat. Carla had her back to me choosing a place on the log to sit. "Carla" I said, and when she turned toward me I opened my arms, inviting her to come into them. She willingly snuggled in and I held her close. I put my hand under her chin, and tilted her face so that our eyes met. The moment was right, the feeling was right, so I released my arms from around her, took her hands in mine and said very softly, "Carla, will you be my wife? I love you so very much and I want to be your husband." She seemed to be deep in thought for a few seconds then said, "Mark, I thought you would never ask. Of course I want us to be married." then with a slight smile, she said, "And we'll have ten kids!" We both laughed and agreed that ten would be a few too many. I added, "So it's settled Carla, we are engaged, right? She came to me again and we sealed our engagement with a kiss that made our future wedding night seem like a distant dream that would never come true. We agreed that we would share the news with our parents, but would wait until graduation before telling anyone else about our engagement.

I spent many hours working on my school assignments. I needed to pass all the classes, so I could have at least two years of college, even if I never attended another class in my life. I realized that there were many things about ranching that I did not know, but figured with some college and as I gained experience, I could handle most problems I would be faced with. Learning the ranching business would have been different if my father was alive, but without him to guide me, I will remember the things I am learning in class and the many things my father taught me, along with some common sense, and hope for success.

I promised Carla that I would call her once every week. We needed to keep our relationship as close as it had become during the holidays, and the weekly conversation helped us to keep that closeness. Since we were engaged to be married, life took on a different meaning as far as our being apart was concerned. Carla was also working endlessly to keep her high grade level at the top, hoping to receive another scholarship. Her parents helped her get settled and boarded their flight to Texas.

Mom, Kati and I were finishing dinner, when the phone rang. Kati rushed to answer saying, "I'll get it Mark, it's probably Sally, she calls me about this time every evening. It's for you, Mark." When I answered, the voice I heard was not a familier one. "Mark, this is Carla's Dad. I'm sorry to bother you, but I needed to make this call without any more delay. I have some terrible news. Carla's Mother and I have been involved in a plane crash, and her Mother was killed. I was slightly injured, but have been released from the hospital and will be okay, but her Mother didn't make it through the crash. Carla told us about the engagement, so I know how close you and Carla are. I felt sure you would want to be with Carla, and also it will help me out." The shock of what Mr. Nelson told me, was overwhelming, I couldn't think for a few seconds, then answered, " Oh sure, I will get to Missoula as fast as I possibly can. I'll take care of her Mr. Nelson, don't worry I will take care of Carla." He said, "She has no one at home, as the rest of our small family are away on a vacation, and I haven't been able to contact them yet. I can't say how soon I will be back home. Possibly tomorrow, it may even be the following day. There are some things here I have to take care of. I want to accompany my wife's body back, so it depends on how things work out here. By the way, I am in Salt Lake City. You may leave a message at the Ramada Inn,room 301. The manager will see that I get any calls or messages that come. Good luck Mark, and I do appreciate your help. When I went back to the dinner table, Mom said, "Mark, you are as white as a sheet. What is wrong?" "Very bad news Mom,Carla's parents were in a plane crash and her Mom was killed. That call was her dad. He was slightly injured, but will be okay. He needs me to go to Carla, give her the terrible news, and get her back here. Mom, what should I do?" "Well, son, you must get started now without wasting a single minute! Give me Carla's number and I will call and tell her you are coming, but will not tell her the reason. Just that you needed to talk to her about something very important, and will be there in the morning. I'll pack a change of clothing while you put gas in the car." I appreciated my mother taking charge and leading me through this time when I was too upset to do it by myself. Missoula is a bit over five hours away, so with a couple of rest stops, I can be there before Carla leaves for school. Night driving is easier, as there is less traffic. I may take a short nap when I stop to rest.

When I was leaving, Mom warned me to be careful and said, "Here is some cash; you will need it for food and gas." I was right about night traveling. I hardly met any traffic until I was into the city limits of Missoula. I pulled into a rest area and took a couple of naps during my drive; probably slept about two hours. Overall I had a good drive. Carla's apartment was near the campus, but when I drove by I didn't see any signs of movement, and realized I was too early to go to her door, so I decided to get some breakfast at a little café where Carla and I had eaten the last time I visited her. I was hungry after the long drive, so the ham and eggs I ordered tasted great.

When I rang the doorbell, Carla answered right away. She was expecting me as Mom had called and told her I was coming. We greeted each other with a big hug and kiss, then she backed off and said, "Okay Mark, why the big rush, an overnight drive? It must be really important. Is our engagement off? What is it?" "No Carla, nothing like that. Something very bad has happened, you will need to be sitting down when you hear it. " I led her to the small couch, took her hands in mine and began. "Carla, there is just no easy way to tell you this, but I had a call from your Dad late yesterday afternoon." She was already looking at me with fear in her eyes. "Your parents were in a plane crash yesterday morning somewhere in the mountains between Salt Lake City and Denver, Colorado. Are they alright Mark, give it to me straight. Are they Okay? Come on, tell me!" "Carla your father is fine, except for some minor injuries. I hesitated before continuing. "Is my mom okay too?" "No Carla, your mom didn't make it." "Are you saying my mom is dead Mark, is that what you are telling me?" I saw the complete shock on her face, then what I had told her became real. She screamed and screamed some more. She ran towards the door, opened it like she was going out into the hall, crying, "What will I do without my mom? I need my mother!" I pulled her from the door, steadied her with my arms and led her back to the couch, encouraged her to sit down, and cradled her in my arms. She finally settled down to heavy sobbing. I continued saying anything I could think of that might calm her down. I thought my presence would ease her grief, and it did. After long minutes of holding her close she spoke in an almost inaudible voice, "Mark, I'm so glad you're with me. I couldn't take this without you."

The phone rang, and when I answered, it was Carla's father. He said, "How is she doing, Mark?" " I think she is calming down a bit now, but it was really, really bad when I first told her. So what are your plans Mr. Nelson?" "I am to meet my wife's parents tomorrow here in Salt Lake, and we will fly to Missoula, with the body, which will be flown to Cody then taken by motor to Powell. I will pick up my car which is parked at the Missoula airport and come straight to Powell. Please take Carla home and stay with her until we arrive. It will mean so much to me to know that you are with her. I realize you have your farm work, but perhaps your man on the ranch will take over for a couple of days. Carla needs you Mark." I assured him I would be more than glad to follow through with his plan and that I could never leave Carla while she is trying to cope with this terrible tragedy. After all, she will be my wife someday, and I love her with all my heart.

Carla did not wish to be alone, even for a minute, so I prepared to sleep on her couch, but many times during the night, I heard her sobbing, and went to her side. When morning came we packed a suitcase with necessary clothing, called her counselor at school to let him know why she would be unable to attend classes for an extended period, and started home. We took our time on the drive back; even stopped for a bite to eat and relax before continuing the trip. As time passed Carla cried a bit less, although occasionally she could no longer hold back the tears. Gradually her tears would fade away. I encouraged her to think about the horses; anything to get her mind off her mother's death, even for a few minutes. As we came near her home, Carla surprised me by asking, "Mark, I'm sorry, but I don't think I can go into my home. Not without my family. Can I go home with you?" "Of course," I said. "Mom and Kati will welcome you with open arms and do everything possible to make you comfortable." "Thanks so much, Mark." She was sobbing again. I pulled to the side of the road, parked the car and took her in my arms as I had done so many times these past two days

Carla spent two nights in our home. Kati and Mother treated her as family, and she seemed to feel the need to be with them. Her father and grandparents arrived the second day of her stay with us. The reunion with her father was an emotional time. Mother, Kati and I were deeply touched by the reunion of two people who shared such grief. Her grandmother had lost a daughter, she too was beside herself with sorrow and grief, but regardless of her own sadness, she opened her loving arms to to Carla.

I visited Carla every day, and I could see that she was gradually getting herself back to a normal life, after the death of her mother. She was very close to her grandparents and loved having them live with her and her Dad. Mr. Nelson returned to his work as manager of J.C. Penny store a week after the funeral, and seemed to be adjusting to living without his wife satisfactorily. The decision to return to college and finish the term was not an easy thing for Carla to do. Two weeks passed and she still could not face going back to her apartment alone. She realized the importance of getting back to classes, but she needed the closeness of her family. After another week and still she seemed no closer to going back to school, her grandmother said, "Carla, I understand how lonely you would be all alone in that apartment, so how would you like for me to go back to Missoula and keep you company for a week or maybe two weeks?" "Oh Gram, I love you, love you, love you! I will be delighted to have you with me. Can you be ready to leave by Sunday? If you can, so will I. Oh Gram, we will have so much fun." Her father said to me later, " Now that sounds like my little girl. I think she is going to be alright now." I heartedly agreed that she was beginning to sound like the girl I'll take for my wife soon.

It is only one day before Mr. Nelson will drive Carla and Grandmother to Missoula. I had a plan and hope it works. I called Carla and when she answered I said, " Hey Carla, I have a message for you from Sapphire and Harmony. They would love to have a visit from you before you leave tomorrow. They will be waiting for you about two o'clock, all saddled and ready to take you for a ride!" "Oh Mark, I can't resist an invitation like that! Tell Sapphire and Harmony I'll be there. Am I supposed to ride two horses at one time, or is there a guy out there who will join me?" "I know a guy who says he loves you. Can he go along and ride Harmony?" When we finished our conversation, I knew I had the Carla back that I had loved so many years.

Early spring brings life on the ranch to non stop proportions. Often it's difficult to decide what takes priorty. The cattle and sheep or field work. Tony and his helpers do a great job, in the field, but I need to check their work and give instructions. Last but certainly not least is the calving, which is a responsibility that my father took care of, and which I am trying to do with very little experience. I call on our faithful Vet often and he leads me through a problem or comes to my aid with a 'house call' that normally an experienced cattleman would be able to do without calling a veterinarian. Doc Lee knew my father many years and is glad to help me when I need him. So far this season the mother cows have had their babies without any problems, but calving season is just beginning, so I'm sure I will need to call the Doc sooner or later. Every time I have Doc Lee out I watch him carefully and learn how to handle these emergencies. As the old saying goes, 'live and learn' that saying certainly applies to me, as I try to take my father's place in running the ranch. Surprisingly, Mom knows a great deal about ranching, and helps me in many ways.

The first few years my parents were homesteading, mother spent the long summer days alongside my dad working in the field. When she talks about those days of driving tractor or hauling a load of grain to town, I find it hard to picture her out there doing such jobs. But she remembers those as the 'good old days' and claims they were happy times. The life of a farmer's wife during homesteading days was not an easy one. Most wives were young and besides doing farm work, they were having babies. During pregnancies, the outside work for a woman stopped. Husbands were thoughtful of their wives condition, and treated them with the utmost respect.

Chapter 18
GRADUATION

TIME FLIES when a person is leading a busy life, as I am these past few months. I am meeting most of my classes, and doing some serious studying at night. I am determined to graduate with an AA degree in agriculture. I realize if I want that diploma I have to study more than some of my classmates who seem to pass a quiz, or write an essay without hitting the books as much as I do. Some people think that getting an AA degree is next to nothing compared to a BA from a four year college, but I am proud to be gaining much knowledge from my classes in community college. I hope to put the things I am learning to work, and become a better rancher as a result of having an AA degree.

Graduation exercises passed without a lot of 'hoop-la'. Kati and Mom attended, along with Tony and his family, and our good neighbors Abe and Mae. I was surprised to have Carla's father and grandparents in the audience. They congratulated me and were sorry Carla could not be there, but she has a few more days left before she will be home for the summer. I had all the support I wanted or needed to make my graduation night special. I saw Lisa with her new boyfriend across the auditorium. She gave me that smile and waved, as if to say. " You were right Mark, I do have a boyfriend that I care for more than I ever did for you!" I felt no jealously, just good riddance. Mom served delicious ice cream and my favorite cake, "Devil's Food" to Tony's family, Abe and Mae, and Kati and me.

Now that Carla was out of school for the summer, we spent hours everyday with Sapphire and Harmony getting them ready for the Fourth of July Fair race. We set a schedule and tried to stick with it faithfully. Carla came at one o'clock every afternoon, and she and Kati worked with the horses until around four o'clock. By four o'clock both Carla and Kati were tired and the horses needed rest. They were watered, groomed, and fed, before leaving them to do whatever horses do to rest. Each day Carla and Kati reported great progress was being made. Sapphire's timing was somewhat faster, but Harmony had a long way to go in order to win a race. Of course Carla was also coaching Kati on her riding skills. This will be Harmony's first race and only the second time for Kati to Jockey. I dropped in at the arena occasionally between work in the field and checking on Tony and his helpers with their irrigating, and weeding. Some fields had to be weeded by hand, and others were done with machinery. I was hesitant to trust the cultivating to anyone other than myself, as it is a tedious job. I remember my father did not allow me on a cultivator until I was a senior in high school, and even then, he kept a close eye on me, in case I veered to one side or the other and chopped some of the plants. My mom told me of an incident that happened in the days when she was doing some field work. She insisted to my Dad that he should let her try to run the cultivator. He agreed to give her a try, but had an eye on his little helper most of the time. She suddenly looked away to wave at him. The tractor veered and she cut down over half a long row of beans. Needless to say, my mother did not help with tractor work after that experience.

When I looked toward Heart Mountain, "my mountain," as I often refer to it, all I could see was a huge cloud of dust slowly heading toward the ranch. The wind was blowing harder than it had been all day, and was getting stronger by the minute. I stopped what I was doing and headed for the corral, to fasten gates and doors that were not on the lee side of the wind. I waved to Tony and his helper to quit the job they were doing, and go home. He too, had felt the wind and dust and realized a windstorm was coming in, so he waved to his helpers, by raising his crossed arms, high in the air and pointing to the sky. Unlike tornados or cyclones; the sky does not give any sign of an impending storm. It simply is hidden behind clouds of dust. Only one year ago, a Wyoming wind storm actually blew a large semi-truck over on its side. The same storm struck a parked airplane, picking it up, and landing it across the run -way; naturally destroying the plane. We do not take these winds lightly, as they can cause serious damage. Not only to crops, but buildings as well. When we sat down for dinner, I could see concern on Mom's face; she recalled to Kati and me how winds such as this one brought disaster to several farmers in years past. She said, "I think this wind deserves our prayers, asking God to protect our ranch, and the farms of our neighbors from any damage this awful wind might do." My mother was a firm believer in prayer, as was my father, and they set a good example for Kati and me. The wind continued at a high velocity. We went to bed feeling like we had everything buttoned down that could be, and except for little creeking noises occasionally I dropped off into a deep restful sleep. When I arose, I quickly dressed in the usual garb for changing irrigation water; which I did each morning before returning to the house to have breakfast I pulled my rubber boots on and headed for the old farm pickup truck, but when I looked toward the machine shop, I stopped short! Something did not look right. Then I realized what was missing. One of the three large storage bins was gone. I looked a bit farther and there it was. It had blown at least a hundred yards from where it stood alongside two other bins. These bins are used for storing grain or beans or any crop that will not sold until after harvest, usually sometime before spring. Apparently, the door to this particular bin was not fastened securely and the wind simply grabbed that bin and destroyed it. Oh well, it's only a crop bin. It could have blown the roof off the barn, or something much more costly than a metal bin. Both the other bins were filled with grain, or I might have seen all three bins in the ditch! I told Mom about the bin, and she remembered a time several years ago when the wind blew one of our bins away, and several of our neighbor farmers lost much of their crop also. The beans had been cut and were lying in rows, waiting to be harvested, and a very strong wind blew the dried beans out of their rows, scattering them, causing at least a fifty percent loss of their crop.

Mom and I felt very blessed that we had an excellent crop this year. We paid all our bills, including Kati's hospital costs, with a few hundred dollars left. We still had our cattle to market, which should bring us a goodly amount of cash. We had followed in my father's footsteps. We did many things we had observed from watching and listening to him make difficult decisions. I am satisfied that he would be proud to know how well our first year without him turned out.

The Fourth of July Fair was only one week away, and we had worked hard getting our horses in shape to enter the most important race in these parts. The one necessary part of our training left is taking Sapphire and Harmony to the race track in town, so they can become familiar with the area and track where they will be competing. Getting the horses to town means loading them in a trailer, hauling them to the track, loading them in the trailer again to spend the night in Carla's lot in town. After spending the night in Carla's horse lot, we practice again the following day. We will do this on Wednesday and Thursday, bring them back to the ranch to our arena, time them each day for speed, then haul them back to the fair grounds early Saturday morning for the big race. Carla feels sure Sapphire will win this year, as she did last year. Kati realizes that this is Harmony's first race and only her second time to jockey, so She will be happy if she places, but is more than happy to have the experience of riding Harmony in his first race.

At last the big race is on in full swing. "Billy the Bully,"will not be entering, as he received a two year sentence in the state prison for stealing Harmony, so we will not have to compete with his horse, 'Trigger."

This is the day! We have never entered two horses before, so our excitement is double what it has been in the past. We tried them out on the track three days ago, and Sapphire especially performed better than I expected, while Harmony looked good we don't hope for her to win. If she performs like she did in practice, perhaps she may make it to third or fourth place, but she will have the experience and if she continues in the path she is headed; hopes are high for a big win in the future. Harmony has many qualities of both her mother and dad. Nochi was a winner in his time and Sapphire shows signs of being a great winner also. Harmony is from a good stock of racers, and it is obvious from the way she is running. I am certain if Nochi had not been injured in a barn fire, he would still be out there running and winning!

Many of Carla's high-school friends were in the grandstand to cheer her on, as well as her Dad and grandparents. Kati did not have as large a cheering section as Carla, but she had a few friends. Several of our ranch neighbors came, and of course Mom and me. All through the grandstand were small groups of people who came to cheer for their favorite horse. Park County Wyoming covers a large area, and the fair is attended by people far and wide. Horses will be entered from towns as far away as one hundred miles. The horses were impatiently waiting for the flag to go down. Jockeys could hardly hold them back. The horses were no more impatient than their jockeys. Everyone in the grandstand was clapping and waving for the race to start. At last the flag came down and they were off. I knew the horses and I knew the jockeys, so I could almost judge what was in their heads. Carla was holding Sapphire back; planning to give her the reins towards the end of the race. Kati was watching Carla from the corner of her eye, and trying to do everything Carla was doing, so she also held Harmony back. In my judgement she should give Harmony a little nudge in the flank and get her up to speed. There were three other horses that took the lead. One of the three that were in the lead belonged to a friend that was in an agriculture class with me in college. He called his horse "Mr.Ed" after the popular T.V. show. Mr Ed had won numerous races in the area, including the Park County Fair race. Mr. Ed. and Trigger had been strong competitors. Mr. Ed was showing his strength and speed in this race as never before. Sapphire lagged behind a bit and to my surprise Harmony was moving up. She was now among the leaders and now close to the lead. My thought about Kati nudging Harmony to move up could only have been ESP working between Kati and me, as the very moment I had that thought, Kati started moving up! it took a little nudge in the flanks to urge Harmony into the speed she was now in. Kati had her head down talking to Harmony constantly; "Come on baby, we can do it, let's show them what you've got. Go, go, go." The finish line was only a few feet away, when Mr. Ed suddenly slowed, giving Kati the lead. She crossed the finish line, and the flag went down simultaneously. I could not have been more shocked. Harmony had won her first race. The crowd went wild with clapping and cheering. My little sister had ridden Harmony to a win. She was a natural jockey. In the meantime, I looked around and saw Mr. Ed with a slight limp as if his ankle was sprained. The pain must have been terrific, causing him to drop back, enabling Kati and Harmony to win the race. Carla brought Sapphire in for third place. After I joined her to take the reins and lead Sapphire back to the trailer, she went straight to Kati and Harmony. They were still receiving congratulations, and were presented with a large arrangement of roses. Mom was there to give her a hug and kiss, but most appreciated was Carla's acceptance of the win. She was overjoyed; after all she was Kati's mentor. Sapphire is a great race horse, but Harmony is even better. If Harmony wins in a regional race like the one at the Billings State Fair, she will step into some big time racing. When I think big time, I am not thinking of a horse like Secretariat, that was born at Meadow Farms in Virginia, but I vision races in our area. Places like the Wyoming State Fair, Cheyenne Frontier Days, or neighboring states. I quote my father who said, " It doesn't hurt to dream, but don't live your life on dreams alone."

Harmony and Kati had earned their way to The Montana State Fair, and we will be there! As for winning, I have doubts that it will happen, but I must let Kati believe that since winning is our goal, we will spend the next two weeks working with Harmony, to keep her in shape for the big race in the hopes that we will reach our goal. After Harmony's performance at the fair, I know I can expect more of her than I ever could of Sapphire or Nochi. She has racing in her blood and it shows.

Chapter 19
The Big Race

WHEN CARLA and I talk about the future; our marriage, children, her education, or any number of subjects that pop up in our conversations, the one fact that is difficult to speak about is her education. She does not want to leave her family and go back to Missoula. One possibility is for her to attend Wyoming State University in Laramie, which is much closer to home. In fact if she arranged her classes to have Monday free, she would be able to drive home Friday morning and return Monday afternoon giving her the equivalent of three days at home. We discussed this plan with her Dad and being so lonely after the death of his wife, he welcomed the thought of having his daughter home more often, and agreed that it sounded like an excellent idea. Of course there would be storms occasionally that would keep her at school, but for most week-ends the plan would work. He felt that

she needed a new car and agreed to trade the old car in
and buy a new one. Both Carla and I were thankful
that he cooperated in the plan so generously. As for our
wedding date; it would be postponed a few months or
perhaps even a year. We would honor her vow to herself
and her parents that she would remain a virgin until we
were married. We loved each other so much we needed
the closeness that intimacy would bring, but we had
made an agreement to honor Carla's vow and we hon-
ored it faithfully. Due to our engagement I had taken
the same vow. True love is not an easy street, as I soon
learned in dealing with our engagement.

Mom, Kati and I were having dinner when there
came a knock on the door. I answered it, and to my
surprise there stood neighbor Abe. We had not seen him
and Mae since the celebration of my graduation, when
they joined us for cake and ice cream. I invited Abe to
come in, and Mother asked him to join us for dinner.
He declined, saying, "No thanks, we just finished
dinner at home. I apologize for interrupting your meal,
but I wanted to come by at a time when I figured you
Mark, and your Mother would both be here. Mae and
I are going to retire to a place in town, and I wanted
you folk to be the first to know. Mae has not been in
good health lately, and also the wind storm the other
day caused us to make the final decision to move. As
you have probably heard, that wind dealt us real havoc.
It did not completely blow the roof off, but damaged my
barn to the point that I would have to build a new one
if we stayed on here. Hundreds of shingles from the roof

are gone, and well, the whole building suffered damage. We will sell the place and wanted you people to have first chance to buy it. The fact that our land joins makes a perfect set up for you. That is if you plan to stay on here. 'young 'punks' like you, Mark, can experiment with all that new technology out there and fly with it. Just wanted to give you first chance to buy before word gets out that it's for sale." Mother l I were both in shock, as we never dreamed that Abe and Mae would be leaving. Of course Abe was several years older than my parents at the time of homesteading. A few years can make a big difference in ones ability to take on the hard work and set backs that often come along with the business of farming and ranching. Mother replied to his offer first, " Abe, I had no idea you and Mae were planning to retire to town, and you will certainly be missed by those of us who are left out here. Goodness, so many are selling their farms and moving to town, but we do appreciate you giving us the news before someone else grabs your place. I agree it is a perfect location for us, and would be an ideal place to add to what we now have. Mark and I will definitely give it a lot of thought, and let you know in a few days. Thanks so much Abe. Please tell Mae I will talk to her soon." Abe left and Mom and I just stared at each other without speaking. We both knew that getting Abe's place was a dream Father spoke about often. "If old Abe would just 'throw in the towel ' up there, we would have more pasture land and eventually buy more cattle." The business end of a transaction like buying Abe's farm would involve more people than

Mom and me. We would be dealing with lawyers, bankers, loan officers, and lastly a title company. Kati was listening intently to our conversation with Abe, and when he left, she brought up the fact that she should be in on the decision also. So Mother said "Well Kati what do you think about buying another farm?" Kati spoke up and said, "It's up to you two. I say buy it." Without giving a reason or carrying the conversation any further, she headed for the living room to watch a T.V. show. I looked at Mom and we both grinned at how nonchalant Kati was about this very important decision we were trying to make.

Mother called Abe and told him we had decided to purchase his farm, which included a small house just the size for a couple of newly weds. The house was built in the late fifties or early sixties. Since Abe and Mae did not have children, they had chosen to build a small, efficient and actually a very attractive little home. Mom asked Abe some pertinent business questions regarding the crops that were already planted, irrigation ditches and actual acreage. She told him we would be in touch at a later date, when we were ready to close the deal. She had been at Dad's side when he purchased other nearby farms, and knew the process of buying land quite well. "Mom, I'm here if you need me, but I will leave the business end of this deal up to you. I may need to co-sign some papers, or if you would feel better I will be glad to accompany you to the bank, please let me know."

When Harmony was entered in the Montana State Fair horse races, two vehicles were taken. I drove my pick-up truck, pulling a horse trailer loaded with a valuable horse, so I left very early, in order to have plenty of time to groom and exercise Harmony before the race. Mother and Kati started much later. Kati was dressed in her 'jockey outfit.' "She and Mom would pick Carla up in town, and the three of them planned to meet me at the sheds where horses were kept until time for the race to start. I agreed to enter the Billings race; not hoping to win, but to reward my little sister for the excellent job she did with Harmony at the county fair race. I knew without a doubt that Mr. Ed would have won, had he not sprained his foot. The fact is, that Kati did a wonderful job of riding Harmony to the winning place, and I felt she deserved to use the skills she had learned again. There was a completely different atmosphere in the grandstand at the Billings fair than we had for the race at home. Unlike a small community, most people were strangers to each other. Money was involved, rather than friendships. Very little cheering took place. Harmony was unknown to racing fans, so very few bets were placed on her. As before, Harmony was eager to get started; Kati loves to ride, so the two of them were edgy for the race to get started. The flag went down, and the race was on. Carla, Mother and I watched with bated breath, fearing Kati would lose her nerve. That never happened and she used all the skills Carla had taught her. Harmony was outstanding, Kati was outstanding, but they lost to a much more experienced horse. They came in at third, which was the same as Sapphire did one year ago. Our family rushed out to congratulate "my baby" as Mother still calls Kati. She did a great job as did Harmony. We could not have been more proud.

Chapter 20
THE HUNTING TRIP

CARLA IS happily situated on her new college campus. So far, she likes it very much. She claims the classes are easier than Montana University, but expects them to be more difficult as time goes by. She has a long drive from Laramie, Wyoming to home, but says she enjoys driving and the thought of being with loved ones will make the drive seem shorter. Marriage plans keep coming up more often these days. Carla and her mother talked about such things long before we were engaged, and now that she can no longer confide in her mother, she and I are talking "wedding." A Christmas wedding has been a dream of Carla's since she was a little girl. Will that dream come true this year, or will she have to wait another year? If we wait one year then graduation would only be a few months away. No doubt the wedding will be a big affair. My mother has offered to help Carla and her grandmother with the planning and preparation, which they accepted graciously. When my mother made the offer, Carla thanked her with an open heart. "Yes, please do, we need all the help we can get." Even though the marriage will not be for months, planning has already begun.

Dinner this evening was an eventful time. Mom announced that she had seen the banker and talked to Abe about finalizing the purchase of his farm. It seems that everything was going our way. We were adding more farm and pasture land and also gaining a small house. Carla and I had never discussed where we would live, but during the thanksgiving holidays I planned to bring the subject up. She had never lived on a ranch, but considering the love she had for animals, especially horses, I was hoping to continue living on the ranch. The house we were buying from Abe would be a perfect home for us. Some paint and new carpets and it could be turned into a comfortable, attractive home.

Riding was my hobby and relaxation. I rode Sapphire one day and Harmony the next day. My riding sessions offered me peace of mind and time to think about future plans for the ranch life I had chosen. When I looked at Heart Mountain, I could see a smattering of snow at the very top, reminding me that regardless of the beautiful fall weather we were experiencing now, time was running out, and winter winds would be blowing, bringing cold to numb our bones. Time to bring out heavy clothing and make sure water pipes were deep into the ground. I imagined Heart Mountain was showing me it's serious side, with staring eyes and a tangled unkempt beard, as opposed to the uplifting smile spread from ear to ear. Regardless of the time of year, as a young boy I had always enjoyed that beautiful mountain; letting my imagination run wild.

My father started allowing me to accompany him on his yearly hunting trip when I was about ten years old. I was too young to shoot a gun, but I rode along, carrying binoculars and chattering incessantly as boys often do at the age of ten. This year would be no different, except I invited a former school chum to join me. I met Kevin in agriculture class in college. He was also interested in ranching, so we enjoyed many visits about our farm life. Kati begged to go hunting with us. "Mark, you know very well I can handle a gun, because Dad taught me about gun safety two years ago and then backed down and wouldn't let me go. I want to go. Please, please. I promise to keep my mouth shut, and will do my share around camp." With all the begging she did, I finally consented to take her along. The wind had not been blowing, except for a breeze now and then, so I disregarded the face of the old man of the mountain. We loaded up our camping gear, along with four horses which included Sam the pack horse. Kevin carried his horse and the pack mule in his trailer, along with some saddles and gear. Kati and I had the rest of the gear and our horses. We headed for the high mountains intent on bagging ourselves a Deer. I left Tony in charge with instructions to ask Mother if he needed advice about anything.

It was a happy time. Kati and Kevin immediately became friends. We parked our trucks in an area several miles down from the campground where Dad and I had spent so many happy days. We unloaded the horses, saddled them, packed our gear on old Sam, our pack horse, carried some sleeping bags and guns with us on our horses and headed up the mountain toward the campground. The ride was even more beautiful than I remembered. Leaves of every color imaginable were falling, squirrels scampered to hide their winters supply of food in fallen logs or under old stumps of trees and as we came nearer to our camp, we spotted deer running deep into the woods when they sensed that horses and people were getting too close. High above the tree tops we spotted a flock of geese overhead going to their warm southern climate.

Kevin had his own cozy little pup tent, and Kati and I shared the tent my Dad and I slept in, which was made for two sleeping bags. Our food was securely stored to keep hungry bears from scaveging our food supply. Not only would bears tear up a camp, but they can be dangerous to people as well.

The first day of hunting, we rode or walked miles looking for an elk or deer, but only saw about three deer among the trees; nothing to shoot at. By the end of the day the three of us were very tired, and Kati was completely exhausted. We opened a can of beans along with a hot dog, swallowed our food like ravenous wild animals and retired to our sleeping bags. Morning came, and we welcomed another day with high anticipations.

Today was the day we would be lucky. I noticed that Kati didn't show the enthusiasm she had yesterday, and she finally said, "Mark, I think I will hang around camp today. This hunting business is for tough people and I guess I am not tough enough. I will be content to go for a walk, read the book I brought. Later I can build up the campfire and cook those steaks we brought. How does that sound?" I tried not to show my relief, but I was glad she was staying in camp. I said, "Sounds okay to me Kati. We'll be looking forward to those steaks. Kevin spoke up and said, "Oh no, Kati, I enjoyed your being with us yesterday, won't you change your mind and come along?" I felt like saying, "No Kevin, you idiot, we are better off without her. Please don't beg her anymore!" I gave him the 'no no' sign with the look on my face, so he backed off. That incident was my first clue that Kevin might be interested in 'my little sister' as a girl friend.

After another unsuccessful day of hunting, and we came within sight of our camp things looked unusually quiet. No fire was burning, and we didn't smell those steaks cooking. As we came nearer, I called Kati's name. There was no answer to my calls. "Kati, where are you, if this is a joke, come out! Kevin was walking the outskirts of the camp, also calling her name. By this time, both Kevin and I were puzzled and apprehensive. Feelings of fear for her safety were beginning to creep into our minds. We knew she had walked instead of riding, as Harmony was grazing peacefully in the area where we kept the horses. We saw no tire tracks, so we knew she had not willingly or forcefully gotten in a car. The best and only thing to do was continue to look, all the while calling her name. "Kati, can you hear me, Kati! Kati! answer me." Dark comes early in the mountains, as the sun does not show its face above the towering trees. The beautiful sunsets we see in the valley, and the big red ball that hovers just above Heart Mountain are shut out by the dense forest. Kati was out there somewhere in the forest. No doubt scared out of her mind, cold and very tired. Kevin and I continued our search until darkness hampered our efforts. We returned to camp and armed ourselves with flashlights and guns. Three shots into the air signaled she had been found, and one lone shot meant that we would return to camp without Kati. Leaving our horses in camp, we each went in a different direction, being very careful to take a path made by hunters over the long period of years these mountains had been tread. After about two hours of looking with a flashlight and calling her name, I heard the one shot I did not want to hear meaning "let's give it up until morning." The November air had a crispness that chilled to the bones. We built a fire and waited out the night. Often dropping into a restless sleep, but always listening for a sound or call that might lead us to Kati. When daylight crept in over the tall stalwart trees of the dense forest we saddled our horses and started out. Kevin in one direction and I in another. After riding until the sun was high above the trees, I heard the shots I was waiting for. Kevin was signaling the good news or possibly bad news that Kati had been found. I hurried back to camp; holding my breath that she had not met with danger. The area in which we were camped was known for its bear population, but as long as food was hidden and experienced hunters had their guns with them, bears did no harm. Kati did not have a gun, she was not on a horse, she wandered off into the woods alone; my imagination was running wild.

I heard voices long before they arrived. Kati was riding behind Kevin and a Forest Ranger was with them. He found Kati sitting under a tree, about five miles from our camp, half asleep; scratches and bruises over her body, but alive. I ran to help her down from the horse, and held her close. I thanked God over and over for saving my sister from harm.

Kati whispered, "Mark, I should have listened to you and stayed home with Mom." We invited the Ranger to stay for breakfast, which he did. Kevin cooked a great hunter's meal; fried potatoes with steak and eggs. Kati tended her small wounds, then sat comfortably in the only folding chair we brought along, wrapped in a blanket. She never asked to join Kevin and I on a hunting trip again!

After the sumptuous breakfast, Kevin and I saddled the horses and headed out for another day of hunting. Before we left we warned Kati to stay close to camp, and she enthusiastically promised to do so.

We had ridden about two miles from camp, admiring the beauty of the tall trees. We saw squirrels making their way to places where they stored food, then I spotted it! An elk for heavens sake. Right there before my eyes, within shooing range. "Kevin" I spoke in a very low voice. "Look, do you see what I see?" He looked in the direction I was pointing and there stood the elk. I never dreamed of getting an elk, I was thinking with good luck we might bag a deer, but here we were looking at an elk that was easily within our shooting range. Both of us took aim and shot in seconds of each other. Kevin's two shots did not put it down, so I shot again and it fell. We were off our horses in no time and running toward where it lay. The next thing was gutting our game. Elk and deer need to be gutted within minutes after they are shot, or the meat will not be good for eating. Elk meat is very much like beef. Much tastier than deer meat. Another name for elk is 'Wapiti,' a name that means elk in a tribal Indian language. The hunting trip was successful. We had the game we came for, we had enjoyed some beautiful scenery, and most important, my sister was safe and a bit wiser for her experience. We were glad to be home. When the butcher in town is finished with dressing and wrapping the elk, one half will go to Kevin and his family and the other half will be enjoyed by my family and friends. My father's hunting dream was to bring home an elk, but in all the years we hunted, we were never lucky as Kevin and I were on our first trip together.

Two years have gone by with with some amazing changes taking place in our lives. Mother and I closed the deal with Abe, and now have one hundred and sixty more acres added to the three hundred we already own.

We have made plans to plant more pasture land, buy more cattle, and increase the acreage of grain and alfalfa for feeding our cattle. I feel the responsibility more with the added acreage, although Tony has gained much self assurance after two years of being encouraged to act on his own judgement. Which leaves me with more time to spend managing the growing herd of cattle. Carla, Kati and I are still very much involved in horse racing, but keep it on a local level. I am convinced that Harmony and Sapphire could go to any number of the larger, more popular tracks, but betting on races has never been my forte. I may enter my horses in the "Montana State Fair" race, or even the " Frontier Days" races in Cheyenne, Wyoming, but I consider those races low key, compared to Belmont Stakes or the Kentucky Derby. My motto is, "stay close to home and be happy." Sapphire and Harmony are ridden every day, except when the face of Heart Mountain says, "No, not today!"

Chapter 21
WEDDING BELLS

CARLA FINISHED the first term at the University of Wyoming but did not return for the last term. Her father and grandparents objected to her decision, until she shared our secret with them.

We planned our wedding for December 27th. Two days after Christmas. Plans for the ceremony, wedding invitations, the wedding gown, and other details were all taken care of during Carla's Thanksgiving trip home. Everyone pitched in with help and ideas. Choosing materials, and patterns for gowns were left to my mother's discretion. Kati was to be 'Maid of Honor' and high-school friends,Carla had known since elementary school were chosen as bridesmaids. Kevin would be my 'Best Man.' Many decisions had been discussed between Carla and me, long before a wedding date was decided on, such as choice of rings. Carla wanted a lovely gold band instead of the usual diamond ring. I agreed and we decided our bands would be engraved with the words 'love to Carla' and the other read, 'love to Mark'. We agreed at the time of our engagement that the wedding would not be a showy affair, and we made every effort to keep it that way.

Mother did a beautiful job in choosing material for bridesmaid dresses. Each girl made their own dress, and Mom sewed Kati's maid of honor dress. The wedding dress was chosen by Carla and her grandmother from a shop in Billings. We exchanged our vows before two hundred guests, with the Episcopalian officiating. Carla and her parents did not attend a church, so the church and Priest was the choice of her grandparents. A reception was held in the Elks Hall of which both my Dad and Mr. Nelson were members. Food was catered by a local restaurant. Carla and I spent a week long honeymoon in Jackson Hole, Wyoming, skiing, snow-mobiling, and enjoying the activities this quaint little town offered. We returned to the ranch, and moved into the house Mother and I purchased from Abe and Mae. We immediately began painting, carpeting, and making the many minor changes that we discovered each day. In January when the spring session of college began, Carla enrolled in correspondence courses that would eventually lead to a degree from the university in Laramie.

The elk hunting trip that lead to Kati's meeting my friend and hunting companion Kevin, has turned into a serious relationship between the two. Mother and I have great respect for Kevin and his family, and they have a

lot of respect for Kati. Mother and I have observed this
relationship as it became more serious.   Many times
Mom admonished Kati about the late hours she was
keeping, but she continued to spend more time with
Kevin than Mom approved of. Kevin spent two years
at Community College, as I did, majoring in business
management. He now works with his father in the
family hardware store. Hardware stores in a ranching
community such as this are big business. Farmers
depend heavily on hardware stores for many things. So
Kevin's future looks very promising. Kati on the other
hand, will complete her second year in Community
College, and it has been a family dream that she would
continue on to Wyoming State in Laramie.

Carla and I join Mom for dinner one evening
each week, and as usual Kati was out with Kevin, so
it was during dinner that Mom said, "Kati has not
been normal recently Mark, and I am concerned that
her aneurism problem may have returned. She seems
to be unusually tired and sometimes I hear her in the
bathroom coughing or even vomiting, but she always
says she is fine when I speak to her about it. What
should I do Mark?" If your father was alive I could
depend on him to advise me, but now I'm asking you
for help." Some unpleasant thoughts were crossing my
mind, but I wasn't about to let Mom know what they
were. I answered her with, "Mom, it is probably nothing.
You have always been overly concerned when things
happen to Kati. I say, forget it. She will get over it soon,

I'm sure." The discussion ended, but I didn' t put it out of my mind, and I doubt if my mother did either.

Two days later, Carla and I were in the corral brushing the horses, when we saw Kevin's car drive in. Kati was sitting on the passenger side, and they seemed to be deep in conversation. They sat in the car several minutes, then opened their doors, walked around the car, held hands and waved to Carla and me. I knew what was coming, but I had not mentioned to Carla about Kati 's problem. She and Kati were like sisters and I didn't think she would believe me, so I kept it to myself. We exchanged a few words about the horses, Kati patted Harmony affectionately, then Kevin looked at Kati and said, "Kati we need to get on with the news we have." She agreed, and after taking a few uneasy breaths said, "Mark there is no easy way to say this, so here goes. I'm pregnant. We didn't intend for it to happen, but that's all I can say. I can't tell Mother yet, she will go into hysterics, so we're telling you and Carla first. We have no excuses, right Kevin?" Kevin had a look of complete humiliation on his face. His expression showed shock, sorrow, but above all, embarassment. I could not help but feel sorry for the guy. About three years ago, it could have easily been me with the same problem.

Lisa and I were into a torrid affair with no inhibitions, and certainly no birth control. I could not look at Kevin and judge him wrongly. I simply said, "Carla and I appreciate your being candid with us. I believe you do love each other, and that will help you decide on the future. Kevin, my advice is to tell your parents, and you, Katie, need to tell Mom, regardless of what you think her reaction will be." Sunday morning was pancake time for the Mathews family, and Carla and I dropped in for some of Mother's pancakes; Carla left most of the cooking up to me, but I have to give her credit; she is improving, sometimes things are actually edible. But pancakes like Mom makes will take years of practice, and as long as we have Mom around, we will eat her cooking. Kati came down from her room, looking like she had not slept, but forced a broad smile and good morning to us. When Mom finished flipping pancakes, and sat at the table to enjoy her own cooking, she looked at Kati and remarked, "Kati, I think you should have more sleep. You may need to see the doctor and have him do a check up. It has been a while since the last one." Kati saw the worried look on Mother's face and without any hesitation simply blurted out. "Mother I have been to the doctor. Mother, I'm pregnant!" The room was as quiet as a leaf falling to the ground. Tears came to Mothers eyes. She reached for a tissue in her apron pocket and said, "I thought you would never tell me, dear. I was not born yesterday, you know. I had my suspicions a few weeks ago. Naturally I am disappointed in your lack of judgement and complete disregard for the values your father and I tried to instill in you, but I have no choice but to accept it." Tears were now flowing out of control. She asked to be excused and left the room. "I need to dress for church," she sobbed. Kati followed her saying, "Maybe I'll go with you this morning Mom." Kati knew she had hurt Mom badly, as if she had taken a knife and stabbed her in the heart. She hoped going to church with her would help heal the wound.

Chapter 22
MOTHER

LIFE IN our family was moving smoothly. It seemed like a spell of normality Had taken over. The sun rises each morning over Heart Mountain and appears as a big red ball burning in the sky ready to burst into flames, with blue and white clouds ceremoniously drifting in and out of the flaming backdrop. Our lives afforded us happiness beyond what the past few years had been.

Carla and Kati took Sapphire and Harmony out of the corral every day for exercise but more so for their own enjoyment. Arrangements were made to take Sapphire to Mr. Ed, a thoroughbred with a history of winning races. We would have a beautiful colt in a few months. Happiness reigned in our family.

When Kati and Mother entered the doctor's office, she leaned heavily on Mother's arm. Tears were in her eyes. After a thorough examination the doctor looked at Kati and said, "your baby is not showing a heartbeat, Kati, I'm afraid the fetus is no longer alive. How long have you had this pain?" Kati thought carefully before answering him. "Probably about twelve hours, doctor." "Kati, I need to ask you a couple of questions and I want you to answer me truthfully. Have you taken a fall or done anything that might have caused this.? "No, certainly not doctor. I wanted this baby. I have been riding my horse every day after school but I had no problems; I have been riding all my life." The doctor looked at her quizzically, then asked. "Now are you sure that you have not fallen or lifted anything that might injure the fetus?" Kati gave the question a bit of serious thought, then said, "Oh yes, Doctor, I did carry a typewriter up the stairs to my room. Do you think…..?" "Yes, the doctor interrupted, that could very well be the answer we are looking for. Something as heavy as a typewriter could injure your baby." Okay Kati, I will meet you at the hospital tomorrow at two o'clock and we'll fix you up like new again. How does that sound? You have your whole life to have babies Kati. I realize this is upsetting to you and Kevin, but I assure you there will be more babies in the future.

Once each day, without fail, I stopped in what is now Mom's house to have a short visit and see if she needed me to take care of any errands that she might have around the house. As usual I came in the back door, walked in the living room where she was sitting with her head back and eyes closed. I said, "Hey Mom, wake up. She replied, " Oh hello Mark, I wasn't asleep, just deep in thought and memories, I guess. I'm glad you are here, we need to talk again, like we did in the old days before you and Carla were married. You know how much I love Carla, and am so happy for the two of you. You now have your own home and family What I wanted to discuss is all about me for a change. Since you no longer live here, and Kati is away most of the time, I really don't have things to keep me busy.

Cooking about one meal each day, little household chores, and laundry are not enough. I have too much time on my hands for dwelling on memories, and twiddlling my thumbs." She smiled and said," And how many times in your life have you seen me twiddling." We laughed together, then she spoke seriously. "Mark, I was thinking about getting a job of some kind. Extra cash is always nice,   but more important, I would be busy. I need an honest answer, Mark, and your opinion means a lot to me." Actually I was not surprised at her idea of working in town. Carla and I were concerned about her recently, as she was often very quiet; not nearly as cheerful as she appeared to be the past couple of years. Now after three years, her loneliness for my father was taking over again.

My mother was only forty eight years old, and a very young looking forty eight. In spite of her years of homesteading and being a wife and mother, she was an exceptionally lovely person. Mother had beautiful clothes, which she bought when Dad was alive, and applied her make-up in a sensible way that helped her maintain a certain amount of dignity. In other words, she was an attractive lady. "Listen Mom" I said, "I am in favor of you doing whatever it takes to make you happy. I realize that you need something outside of this house to keep you busy, so my advice to you is, go for it. If you can find a job that you like, give it a try." She gave me a hug and said, "Okay Mark, we'll see what happens. Maybe I will become a sales lady, or clean windows in a service station," she said jokingly.

I told Carla about Mother's idea of getting a job in town, and she was all for it. She even said she would speak to her Dad at the J.C. Penny store about Mother working there as a sales-lady. Herb and sometimes Carla'a grandparents were becoming very good friends, and often were guests on special holidays. Mother was famous for her delicious meals and enjoyed having the Nelsons out for dinner. arla loved to try her hand at cooking for these dinners, and of course Mother welcomed having a pie or cake brought in. Herb and Mother had a wealth of experiences to talk about. I figured he would be very happy to give Mother a job if he needed extra help.

It took Mom almost a week to get the courage to actually go to a couple of businesses, and place an application for a job. It had been a period of more than thirty years since she last worked. Her first stop was at the one and only hardware store. She was acquainted with the manager from the many times she had been in to buy something that was needed on the ranch. Secondly she applied in a dress shop. At each place she explained her reason for the decision to work in town. Last she went into the J.C. Penny store and talked to the manager Herb Nelson. Since he knew the circumstances surrounding her decision, he was very understanding, and promised to let her know if he had a vacancy. She now had three applications filed. She drew a sigh of relief and was eagerly looking forward to getting home, kicking her shoes off and having a cup of tea. "What a day," she said to the four walls, "I would not wish to do this everyday!"

A week went by and no calls. "Don't give up, Mom, it's only been one week, and in a small town like ours, jobs don't become available overnight." Carla added, "He's right Ann, you'll get a job when you least expect it!" Carla was right. The following day the phone rang and it was Herb. "Hello Ann, this is Herb at Penny's. Are you still interested in that job you ask about last week?" Mother almost dropped the phone, and had to catch her breath before she could talk. "Oh yes Herb, or should I call you Mr. Nelson? Thank you so much. Your call caught me by surprise, but I certainly do want the job." "Okay Ann, can you start this Monday? One of my younger gals informed me this morning that she is pregnant. She will be here until the end of the week, then I will need a replacement for her, and guess who I thought of right away? So how does Monday sound?" "Fine, just fine Mr. Nelson. What time should I be there?" "Ann, please call me Herb, except when you talk to the other employees. I'll see you Monday, Ann."

Mom was so thrilled she couldn't resist calling us with the good news. You would have thought she was a hungry, homeless person looking for a job. "I feel like celebrating," she said, "How about you and Carla coming down for dinner this evening? If you'll come I will make fried chicken. How does that sound?" "Hey Mom, sounds good to me. We'll be there about six."

Thank goodness, I said to Carla, "Mom is over, the despondent mood she has been in these past few weeks." Mom loved her job at Penny's and especially enjoyed working for Herb. They soon became lunch or dinner companions on working days, but after a few weeks, they were actually going on dates. Mr. Nelson confessed to Carla that being with a woman again was very good medicine for a loneliness he had lived with for three years. Around town they were referred to as that "Penny's man and his girlfriend." A few more weeks passed and that "Pennys man and his girlfriend" were talking marriage. This remark may sound a bit flippant, but it certainly is not. The marriage of our mother and Carla's father was a serious matter. Mother cooked a family dinner for Herb and Carla's grandparents, and of course, Kati, Carla and me. We were having dessert and coffee; enjoying a light hearted conversation, when Mother found a lull in the good humored atmosphere, and said, "Will everyone listen please. Herb and I think it is time for a family talk." She's right," Herb said, "Lets be serious for a few minutes and have that talk." Everyone respectfully laid their desert forks and coffee cups down, in preparation to enter in the discussion. Herb took the lead, "As you kids, 'we were still kids to our families' may have noticed, Ann and I have become more than family friends, we care very much about each other. I guess you could call it love. That's not to say either of us could possibly replace the deep love I had for my wife or Ann for her husband. We realize that could never happen, but we both feel a great longing for companionship. We feel God has his hand in our lives and given us a second love. Namely, each other, although the decision to marry depends on how our children feel about having a step mother and father. A pin could have dropped and no one at the table would have heard it. Mother spoke up and said, "I agree totally with Herb in everything he has just said. I feel he put it in the right words so I have nothing to add." "Kati, what do you think about our marriage?" For once in her life, Kati was struck wordless. Seconds went by, before Kati resplied. "Okay, I say okay. Kevin and I will be married when I finish school and I will be gone. At least I won't be living here with Mother. Looks like she will end up alone in this big house. So I say, do it." "Alright," Mother said, "Kati has spoken her piece, who will be next?" At that point Carla spoke up. "I couldn't agree with Kati more. Her reasoning is logical, and, I would more than welcome Ann as both a mother-in-law and step mother. That is all I can say except I love you both dearly so I say; go for it!" It was my turn now, so I responded with, " I agree with the girls. It looks like an excellent arrangement for everyone involved. " You can depend on me to think about the business end of the marriage. I'm sure you have already discussed the matter between the two of you, but it seems to me that a pre-nuptiol agreement would be a good idea, since you both have homes and other properties. It's just a suggestion 'in case it slipped your minds." "Thanks Mark," Herb said, "You are right. We have not discussed a pre-nuptial, but we surely will take care of it soon."

The wedding between my mother and Carla's dad was a very simple affair with family and a few close friends in attendance. Kati invited Kevin and I asked Tony and family to come. The Honeymoon was postponed until Herbs vacation time; a trip to Hawaii was planned, but for the time being, "Mom and Dad," Mr. and Mrs. Herb Nelson left immediately for a week-end in Billings, Montana,having fun and learning to love again Heart Mountain stood tall and proud, as it had for eons, watching over the valley with a protective force like a mother to her child, always there, but warning if trouble was on the way. The long cold, windy winter was coming to an end. Spring was just around the corner, and farmers returned to their fields getting the soil ready for planting. This time when I gazed up at my mountain, I saw dark clouds hovering over the face of Heart Mountain. I thought, "It's too late for a blizzard. maybe a rainstorm is on it's way." Precipitation of any kind, whether it be rain or snow, is always welcome in a dry climate and more so by farmers and ranchers. I went about my usual chores, feeding and watering the few animals I kept in the corral and barn, when a huge streak of lightening lit up the entire barnyard, followed by a loud clap of thunder. A few minutes earlier I had observed Tony driving a tractor, going from one end of the long field to the other and thinking, "he knows it looks like rain, why is the still working?" I looked again; the tractor was still moving slowly, but Tony was not driving it. I hurridly drove up a side road, ran to the tractor, put it in a fast gear, and drove back up the field, still wondering why Tony left the tractor without cutting the motor off. I did not need to guess anymore. Tony was lying motionless in the freshly plowed dirt.

When I saw him lying there, my legs would not carry me fast enough. The first thing I thought of was that he had a heart attack, but when I saw the burn on the left side of his neck I knew right away he had been struck by the bolt of lightening I heard a few minutes ago. I tried with all my strength and breath to resesitate him, but soon knew I had to get to a phone. I saw a man coming toward us; it was Jose one of our hired men. He saw me driving the tractor recklessly and was hurrying across he field to help, whatever the situation might be. By now the wind was blowing hard and rain was coming down. I tossed him Tony's coat from the seat of the tractor and yelled for him to spread it over Tony's face. My heart was beating faster than I ever thought possible, but I had to get help and fast. When I reached my truck parked in the field road, I turned the tractor off, and ran to my truck. At that point I changed my mind and drove the pick-up as fast as it would go across the field, bouncing over ruts and clumps of dirt, finally making it to where Tony lay, with Jose leaning over him, trying to keep the coat over Tony's face protected from the rain. Jose and I carried Tony to the truck, working as quickly as possible. We placed him in the bed of the truck with Jose beside him and drove to Tony's house, which was closer than mine or Mother's. Maria his wife was looking out the window. When she opened the door I ask her to bring a blanket and call the hospital and let them know we were bringing Tony in. I didn't tell Maria what happened but simply to come to the hospital as soon as she could. We spred the blanket over Tony and wasted no time driving to the hospital. Jose sat in the back with Tony's head on his lap. Hospital staff were waiting when we drove in to the emergency area. It was only after Tony was taken inside that I suddenly realized the shocking and terrible thing that had happened. Tony was struck by lightening and died. My mind could not process the severity of the picture that raced across my mind. I had tried with all my heart and strength to bring him back and failed. Failure is not a word that often pops up in my vocabulary. I can't remember when if ever, I failed at something I was supposed to do. This time I failed. If I had only waved at Tony sooner, before the lightening came, or maybe if I had postponed the tractor work until a few days later. My mind was cluttered with "what ifs?" Tony would still be alive had I made different decisions. This man had been like a father to me from the age of ten years, but now he is gone. Gone from his wife Maria, and the three children he adored. Gone from this ranch he loved. Less than one month ago, I made him happier than a man could be, when I raised his yearly wages and asked him to be the foreman of our expanding ranch. He hugged me and said with tears in his eyes, "Mr Mark, you will never be sorry you are putting your trust in me. I will do my very best." We shook hands over the deal and he hurried home to share the good news with Maria. I used a phone inside the long hallway in the hospital to call Mom at work in the Penny's store. When I started to talk, my voice cracked, tears started flowing, and I found myself unable to speak. "Mom, please come to the hospital now, we need you here. Something bad has happened." I hung the receiver up and found a seat on a nearby bench. My grief was taking over. My legs had no feeling, they were like wooden posts, and I couldn't breathe; I felt a heaviness in my chest, as if I had dropped lumps of coal inside it. I sobbed uncontrollably, my entire body shaking. When my father died suddenly, I was more concerned about traveling to Rochester to be with Mother and Kati, and supporting them in their grief, so I couldn't give in to my own feelings. Grieving for my father crept into my soul slowly; days later, I was hit by a deeper, longing for his presence, but always trying to be brave for Mother's sake. I love Tony as a seond father, companion, and the person I had leaned heavily on for help and advice during these trying times of learning to manage the ranch. He was steadfast in his devotion to his duties. I had lost a devoted friend.

I felt a familiar hand on my shoulder. It was Carla. Mother had called her with the news. She spoke softly, "Mark, I am so sorry. I know you lost a wonderful friend. Your Mom called me after she came to the hospital. She is terribly upset, but is staying with Maria. Please come home with me now. There is nothing we can do here. Tony told Maria years ago that when his time on earth was over, he wanted to be burried beside his parents in Mexico. Lets get Ann and the three of us will 'make a decision about Maria and the children.

Jose and Sarah invited Maria and the three children to spend the night with them. Jose's wife Sarah, was a sister to Maria. The sister's were very close, so we knew Maria would be shown much respect and kindness in their small home.

When Maria returned home from Mexico after her husband's funeral, Mother and I were ready to let her know of our decision to allow her to continue living in the house that had been her home for many years. No money was involved. It would be her home as long as she wished to live there. We also made a gift of the money she borrowed for the trip to Mexico. We were eager to do everything necessary to help her and the three children continue to live comfortably without a husband and father. Tony was a trusted, faithful, friend many years, and if my father was here, I am certain he would do for Marie and her little family the things, or even more for the family Tony left behind.

Carla's grandparents planned to return to Wyoming from their winter home in Texas by early June. Winters in southern Texas draw many "snow birds" as they were referred to by local people in these winter havens. They are retirees who left the cold climate of northern states during winter months, and traveled to warmer places, such as Texas and Arizona.

Herb loved ranch life, so he was happy to lock his house in town up and move to the ranch where he enjoyed helping with chores around the farm on weekends. Mom insisted that she was still young enough to start riding again, so they became avid riders. They purchased a couple of 'Nags' as Carla and I jokingly referred to them, and spent many days riding their saddle horses. No race horses for those two.

Chapter 23
THE CHRISTENING

CARLA'S FAMILY, Kevin and Kati, Mom, Carla, Herb and Maria and children, sat in pews at the front of the church near where the Minister would be performing the Christening ceremony. This was a special day for our families, and everyone dressed in the best for the occasion.

The Minister welcomed the family and guests, then offered a prayer, after which he asked the father to bring the child forward. He took our child in his arms, made a few loving comments about our baby, and then said, "I have been asked by the family to read the following poem."

For Mark:
To welcome a child born of mutual love,
Is truly a blessing sent down from above,
Now that Mark is among us, we share in the joy,
Brought to our lives by this small special boy,
With love in his heart, and light in his eyes,
The family around him will know no goodbyes,
Together with friends who will watch as he grows,
Enveloped with love, that from his family flows.
All our Love,
Mom and Dad

He dipped his fingers into the font and placed his hand on the babies head and repeated :

I now christen you Mark Mathews 11. He held our son up for everyone to see and said, "and now I present Mark Mathews 11". The guests applauded and we formed a family line to receive many heartfelt congratulations.

I would be remiss if I ended this book of memories without again gazing toward Heart Mountain with its majestic beauty as a symbol of strength and courage to everyone in the valley who find comfort, as I do, by her splendor and everlasting watchful presence. We call our Valley "Heart Mountain"!

THE END